The (the Quiet One

SOME HAVE WALKED AS GODS ON THE EARTH.

All the characters in my books are pure fiction.
I didn't think I even had to say this.
I was wrong.

CHARLES "DAVE" COX

Acknowledgements

Short Stories

Prairie Times	June 18, 2011	The White Rainbow
Prairie Times	July 9, 2011	The Bell of Vallecitos
Prairie Times	Aug 17, 2011	Cowboy Billy Meets the Red Cow Disease

Books*

*All of my books can be found on Amazon.com.
*Available in paperback or on Kindle

Life, Cowboys and the Free Press	Red Dashboard Publishing, 2017
Tales From Knob Creek Road	Red Dashboard Publishing, 2018
Much of Nothin' About Ado	Red Dashboard Publishing, 2019
The God Hole of Mescalito	Cox Publishing, 2021
The Baker's Redemption and Other Goodies	Cox Publishing, 2022
F*ck ''Em and Feed 'Em Fish Heads	Cox Publishing, 2024

Awards

Life, Cowboys and the Free Press	Will Rogers Medallion Winner Western Fiction Short Stories, 2018

Dedications

Rebecca Ann Cox

(1957 – 2019)

Where her spirit dwells is now a better place.

If she is not in heaven, heaven does not exist.

She taught me love is enduring and never selfish.

She was my personal gift from God.

J.D. Crider

For sharing his wonderful story about his

kin folks for their part in the creation

of the Great State of Texas.

Table of Contents

The Owl and the Quiet One

Introduction

Thanks and a tip of my cowboy hat to my friend, J.D. Crider, of Arkansas for sharing a great true story about the patriarchs of the Crider family in Texas, J.P. Crider and his full blood Comanche wife, Polina. There already have been stories and songs written about the pair. I thought the account of their lives so interesting I decided to borrow their story to write a fictional account of their extraordinary lives.. My story, characters and incidents are 100% pure fiction. This is one of the many little known events in the history of the founding of the Texas we know today. I admit a certain amount of prejudice on my part after spending forty-five years living in West Texas. God Bless Texas!

The Owl

His Christian name was James Rogers Grinder. His family called him Jimmy. The only ones still alive remembering that name were his dad, his stepmother, and his step brothers and sisters. His mother and his siblings had been killed in a house fire in Missouri, burned by a band of Yankee Red Legs looking for plunder from anyone, friend or foe. After the tragedy his father took up his guns and his son and headed for Texas to what he hoped was an escape from the madness of the Arkansas, Missouri border. He did not know it at the time but he was only leaving one terror for another. He was trading the chance of being murdered by his fellow Americans, Yankee or Confederate, for the very real possibility of being murdered by Mexicans, outlaws, Comanche, Kiowa or Southern Cheyenne.

His father had remarried soon after arriving in Texas to a widow with a farm and no grown men to help. Jimmy grew up on the frontier learning not only the skills of a farmer and rancher but also the added benefit of growing up in the unlimited freedom of the border regions of Texas; for a young man this was the equivalent of heaven on earth. He had the freedom to grow up in a man's world, a warrior's world of weapons, hunting, tracking, horses and fighting. When Jimmy turned seventeen he declared himself a full grown man and left home with the clothes on his back, his horse and tack, his gun, his bow, his knife and his life. He also had one special gift in his saddle bags, a copy of the Bible, the same one his father used to teach him to read and his numbers. His father read from this book by the fireplace every night as long as Jimmy could remember. In the frontier you grow up early and fast or you die.

Jimmy now a man of twenty-four was known to his new neighbors and fellow Rangers simply as, J.R. J.R. was known by the Mexican bandits as, *pinche, cabron. pendajo,* among other profane names they uttered right before they died. The rustlers usually called him, god damn son of a bitch or motherfucker, right before

2

the rope tightened around their necks or the bullet struck their brain or their heart. The Comanches simply called him Owl because he always seemed to know what they were going to do before they did. He was either a witch or an owl. The witch was to be feared but the owl was wise. They preferred to think of him as Owl because a witch was just too terrifying to contemplate.

The Quiet One

The screaming of the thousands of horses being shot in the Palo Duro Canyon was just too much for the young girl. She had run into the brush with her ears covered but it did no good. Her world was dying. She escaped the sights but the sounds followed her for several miles beyond the rim of the canyon. She was leading her favorite pony, Long Walker, who was known for his endurance crossing the plains without water. This was a skill that would be needed in the following weeks as they headed for the Enchanted Rock, a spiritual place of great power for her mother. The Enchanted Rock was five hundred miles across the llano from Palo Duro Canyon. Her mother always told her that if she was ever lost or she became separated from her family by their enemies to make her way to the Enchanted Spirit Rock for guidance and protection. She walked Long Walker as fast as she could trying to distance them from echos of the gun shots and the terrified screams of the horses coming from the walls of the canyon.

Colonel MacKenzie was making sure Quanah Parker's band was going to come in to the reservations. A Comanche with no horse was a different enemy than the one mounted on his war horse. The army not only killed Quanah's horse herd but also destroyed the people's winter supplies of buffalo meat by burning their lodges. The women and children were homeless and had no food for the winter. The only alternative left for the war chief was to bring his people in to the reservation to save them from being exterminated.

The young girl was fourteen winters old. When she was born her mother had named her Little Mouse. Her mother had crept into the brush alone to give birth. As she lay with her new daughter on her breast a field mouse crept out of the brush and began to chew on the umbilical cord before her mom had a chance to cut it with her knife. She whispered to the child, "That is you my sweet girl. You will be my Little Mouse, quiet and always seeking life."

Except for her pony Mouse was alone. She had no idea of what had happened to her father, mother or brothers. She wanted only to rejoin her people but was terrified to turn back because she feared the blue coats would not only kill her but Long Walker too. Long Walker was her horse brother. They had crossed many miles of high plains and deserts together.

She remembered her mother's favorite campsite on the Pedernales River near the Enchanted Rock and all of the good times her family and friends had along the banks of the life giving river. She began to walk with Long Walker in the general direction of her destination. She would ride him later when they would be further away from the blue coat Indian scouts and their prying eyes. Long Walker didn't need to be led. He would follow behind her quietly as long as she needed him to. She was his horse sister. He knew Mouse would take care of him.

Mouse like every member of her tribe knew every water hole in this dry and barren country. The water holes were far and few in this dry arid high plains desert but they were there if you knew where to look. Mouse would survive by eating bugs, small birds or rabbits she occasionally would kill with a rock, there was also berries and other plants she knew she could eat that would not make her sick; for water between the far apart sources she would bite open cactus or drink the morning dew. Long Walker's water would come from the moist pulp of cactus after his horse sister cleaned away the stickers. She would also feed him certain bugs and plants she knew that would keep him alive until she could find the elusive water and grass her brother needed. Long Walker like his sister was a survivor. Mouse walked on moving quietly in the shadows and brush of the plains. If you did not see her coming you would never hear her until she was right there beside you, a quiet phantom appearing out of nowhere. She was in fact, The Quiet One.

When Worlds Collide J.R.

J.R. had been lucky he had lived thru the Lost Valley Fight near Jacksboro led by Major Jones. They had only survived by sneaking out under the cover of darkness. The darkness and the Indians over confidence of victory was what had saved them from losing even more men. J.R. knew that fighting the Indians was a necessary part of settling the frontier if they were ever to live in peace and bring more settlers to Texas. When he first joined the Texas Rangers it was all fun and games for a young man seeking adventure. The more blood that flowed on both sides made this game of life and death a dangerous one, a very dangerous one indeed. As J.R. grew in age and knowledge of the way things really are in the hunting and fighting of other men the more his thoughts turned to finding a wife, settling down and starting a proper ranch. He would always do his duty for Texas but it was time he thought about a future for himself.

He could see an end to the Red River War was coming as more and more of the Indians were being moved to the reservations. His sympathizes lie with the innocent victims on both sides and the Quaker agents who ran the reservations. How do you explain to a pioneer or a Mexican standing over the ashes of what was his home, the butchered remains of his family or his missing children or wife that the fault lie elsewhere. If he were an Indian he would be angry too, seeing his wife and children butchered or starved over a few greedy men in Washington. On both sides remorse, fear and vengeance were all that were on their minds. Emotion rules the mind of man not reason. What a mess!

He wished for once they would send his Ranger Company after the Indian agents in Washington. That would probably do more good quicker than all the fighting they could do out here. A little old fashioned frontier justice was what Washington needed. A few feet burned over hot coals was usually enough to bring anyone around to their senses. He knew these types of decisions were above his pay grade so he would just do what he always did, keep his eyes and ears open, his mouth shut and his mind to the grindstone of the immediate task at hand. Forget to focus on your surroundings out here and you could wind up dead. The frontier had no sympathies for the weak. J.R. prophesied to himself that with the advance of civilization there would be an endless supply of rustlers, whiskey, gun traders and Mexican bandits for the Rangers to pursue. Hopefully, by this time he would be sitting by the fire teaching his own children to read and write by the Bible he kept close.

The immediate duty for his company was scouting the country near the Enchanted Rock and the Pedernales Falls for any strays or survivors from Palo Duro fight or any wild bucks that had ditched the reservation to try and rekindle their old way of life. Their orders were simple: find them, convince them to return to the Indian agents, one way or the other, escort them back to the reservation either willingly or as prisoners.

They weren't to fight unless they had no choice. Talk and promises were the order of the day. How in tarnation were they supposed to talk to Indians who didn't speak any English? They only had two interpreters for the whole company and they were scattered all over West and North Texas. Just like some of the Rangers a few of the Indians did speak broken Spanish so that would help. There was always sign talk but that only went so far.

He wished himself good luck as he gave his horse a kick as he headed for the Pedernales River. This was his assigned area to scout. His company had been divided into one or two men teams with their orders to bring any Indians found to Fort Sill. Some of the men preferred working with a partner while other chose to work alone. J.R. chose to work alone. He knew enough about himself to know he wasn't a coward or stupid.

This was the way he liked it, alone on the plains, no talking, no arguing or agreeing on what to do. When he was alone he was in charge; all decisions and their outcomes were his alone. He knew that out here heroes often died alone and in pain. He was not going to martyr himself if he could help it. If he needed help he would go get it. Easy, peasy, quiet and patience were the order of the day, his orders to himself. If the bands were too big for him to handle he would send word back to the company for reinforcements. Life was simple if you let it come to you instead of forcing it.

Mouse

Mouse had been heading south for almost a month moving in an erratic pattern in her search for the water holes she remembered from her childhood. A good Comanche mother knew to pass this life saving information on to her children. Mouse had to do this while hiding from any others she saw especially if she found the signs of their recent passage. Any humans out here could be a danger, even other Indians. She would know the signs left by her own people. All others were to be avoided. Any enemies could mean: captivity, forced marriage, slavery, rape or death.

Sometimes she could remember the exact location of the watering holes and other times she could not. It was slow work: hiding from enemies, alternately walking and leading Long Walker, searching for signs left by her tribe near watering holes and the constant search for food. Long Walker was her salvation in this journey, her private exodus.

She loved Long Walker like a brother. He was a good listener but she missed human companionship especially her mother. Her brothers she alternately loved and hated her depending on the amount of torment they put her thru. They could really scare her with their cruelty and then the next time be very sweet and bring her honey or flowers. In later life when she had time to dwell on her past she realized the gifts had been apologies for their cruelties. Her brothers were just that way even to their horses, wives, friends and enemies. For now she did not wish to dwell on them because it was her mother she really missed.

Her mother loved her unconditionally. She called her, "my special Little Mouse", when they were alone but only Mouse or daughter when others were present. Her mother taught her everything a young Comanche girl should know to prepare her for adulthood. A Comanche woman was taught how to work hard for her family and her tribe. She taught her how to cook, how to sew, how to work hides properly, how to break and make camp, how to identify plants and about horses.

Her mother was so gentle with horses it amazed her. While many of the braves broke horses into submission her mother would whisper gently while rubbing the horses down. The horses after a while would run to her for these "horse massages". She seemed to push love from her spirit, thru her fingers into the flesh and spirit of the horse. Before long she would be riding the animal, talking to it the whole time with the same words she used when rubbing them down. She taught her daughter that thru her words and hands she could turn the horse into the equivalent of a big puppy. She called it her, "horse spirit."

She often told her daughter how the first horse came to her people and they didn't know what it was and had no word for it so they called it, pia sarii, because they thought it was a big dog. Later when they realized this animal was not a dog but was it's own animal they gave it a new name, puuku. She taught her to love their horses like family. The horses were the key to all of the wealth the Comanche now possessed. Could her daughter imagine moving camp without pack horses with only the women, old people and dogs to carry everything? She hoped those days were long gone. The horses worked, rode the men off to raid, steal and fight. The Comanche was only as good as his horse.

It was not wise for Mouse to dream or think of the past too often when on the trail. Like all the others living on these plains to not be observant and alert could mean death. One day as she rode Long Walker out the mouth of a canyon there it was, the Enchanted Rock. She walked her horse to the summit where she spent a whole day praying and singing before heading off in the direction she knew lay the Pedernales River.

The Education of Mouse

The Owl had learned a long time ago that when working arid country everything and everybody came to the rivers eventually. They had to in order to survive. He needed to water his horse and fill his canteen and if it looked safe enough he would let his horse graze for a while on the rich grasses along the river banks. He watched the Pedernales for a full day before approaching a place he was sure he could hide himself from prying eyes.

Mouse left Long Walker in an arroyo near the river to graze while she crept thru the willows to get herself a much needed drink of water. She had already watered her horse just like her mother taught her. Puuku comes first even before human beings for without puuku we are nothing. Mouse and her horse had both lost weight on this long journey but they had made it. Her skinny face made her naturally large eyes look even bigger.

This was the first thing the Owl saw when he broke thru the willows on the opposite bank to fill his canteen, those large dark eyes surrounded by blue. He had heard nothing. For as long as he lived he could close his eyes and see hers. He had never seen anything like them, black pearls in a sea of blue. Neither were scared, neither moved for what seemed an eternity. This in itself was amazing considering they were supposed to be enemies. In normal circumstances both would have ran off in opposite directions, one to prepare for a fight, one for her horse to run but neither moved until the Owl made the universal hand signs for peace and talk. The Mouse smiled.

Mouse saw a tall white man giving the signs for peace and talk. She could not explain why she did not run. Who knows perhaps she was just following her own calm personality or maybe she was submitting to the human desire for companionship. She was very lonely. Long Walker listened well but was not much of a talker. She just remembered smiling at the man. She felt no fear only being happy to finding another human being.

She was not afraid. She did not move while the white man swam across the river. The Owl held his pistol above his head as he crossed the river. The girl could see his gun but continued to wait patiently for her life to proceed. She felt at peace in his presence.

He was dripping wet. He came to where she was but did not speak. He smiled at her. They stood there two young people not knowing what to say to each other or how to say it. He was looking at her but he was also listening. Listening for the sounds of enemies in the brush.

He was the first to move walking into the willows behind her. He read her tracks until he found her skinny horse grazing. He was convinced the girl was alone. He returned to where he had left her by the river, she had not moved. He made the sign food before swimming back across the river. The Owl returned with his horse and gear and immediately built a small fire. He made coffee and cooked bacon. The girl watched his every move. He made the sign for sit and they sat and shared their first of many meals together.

"You sure are quiet ain't you girl?" She sat there staring not understanding a word. "What is your name?" He made the sign for name. She answered with the sign for small animal. "What animal? I'm not going to call you small critter that's for sure." She continued to smile. "I could call you Blue Eyes or Smiling One but I don't know the sign for those words. You sure are quiet. How about I call you Quiet? I know I'll call you, Quiet One." Owl made the signs for name and quiet. She smiled and let out a laugh. Owl smiled and said, "Well that's it for now I'll call you the Quiet One. That's us, The Indians call me The Owl so we will be The Owl and the Quiet One." He made the signs for his name, Owl and her name, Quiet. This brought laughter from them both. They camped by the river that night.

The next morning as the sun began to rise both were already wide awake. She had slept but as always woke way before the dawn. If she was at home in her family's teepee she would already be preparing the morning meal. Owl had maintained vigilance all night just in case she had friends or family that might show up. "We'll stay here for a few days and let our horses get healthy and try and get some meat on your bones while I figure out what to do. I have orders to take you to Fort Sill so I reckon that is where we will head for." She only smiled. He began to rekindle the fire but she took his hand and shook her head no.

She walked off and returned with an arm load of dry wood for the fire. Owl watched as she made the fire. As soon as the coals were ready he got out his coffee and bacon; again she grabbed his hand, took the coffee and bacon from him, made the signs for me and cook. "You might be handy to have around. I guess I could teach you some white talk." The Owl picked up the coffee and said, "coffee", then he enunciated it slower and pointed to her, "coo....ff.....eeee."

She always smiling said, "cofe."

He laughed, "That's right, cofe." He made the sign for good.

She repeated, "cofe", until he got her to stretch it out until it was as close as she was going to get to its proper form. They repeated the exercise for bacon, fire and water until he was satisfied with her pronunciations. They were happy with each other. The next day and every day thereafter until they reached Fort Sill he would continue her education in English while he learned basic Comanche trying to find out who she was.

Every day as they moved closer to Fort Sill they learned not only more of each others language but at the same time learning about each other. As the Owl drew closer to the reservation a dread came over him. He really liked her. He thought he might actually love her. He had given her a white name, Molly. The name of his late mother. When they were two days out the Owl who now referred to himself as J.R. announced, "Molly, I've made up my mind. I have fulfilled my obligation to the Rangers and I'm going home. If you'll have me I'm taking you to my ranch near Kerrville, Texas. Do not worry girl I am a believer and will marry you legal. I promise to take care of you the rest of your life."

As they detoured toward J.R.'s ranch in Texas it took a whole week for J.R. to get across what he had meant by his speech to her before leaving the Oklahoma Territory. When she finally understand that the Owl now known to her as J.R. wanted to take her to his teepee and become his woman she was happy. She liked him. He was brave and kind. She had no family to worry about bride price so she was free from worry and accepted him as the wife of a white warrior. When she finally put all of the pigeon English, Spanish and Comanche together: she reached out, touched his arm, smiled and made the signs for warrior and woman together under the same roof.

By the time they made it back to J.R's ranch they were like a couple of kids, just being young and in love. J.R. went to town and convinced the Baptist Preacher to marry them. He agreed only if Molly would first be baptized in the river. J.R. explained to Molly that the white medicine man was going to put her under water to become one with the white man's Great Spirit. Molly laughed but agreed to this strange custom. She had her own thoughts about these events but as always kept them to herself. What a strange marriage ceremony to put your wife under water! Maybe they wanted to be sure she was clean. She knew God was everywhere even in the water. If they wanted her to look for God under the water it was good with her.

The scariest part was when the preacher held her under the water. She was close to panicking by the time he brought her up. She did not see their water God but who knows maybe you had to be white to see him. When she was brought out of the water the strange medicine man said a lot of words at her she did not understand but her husband was happy and that was all that mattered. After she had dried herself off with a blanket and handfuls of grass she and J.R. stood by the bank of the river and the strange medicine man said many unknown words at them. When he finished talking J.R. shook the man's hand then the newlyweds got on their ponies and rode back to the ranch to begin their new life together.

Word soon spread that J.R. had returned, quit the Rangers and the strangest thing of all had taken a Comanche bride. There were still a lot of hard feelings, prejudice and animosity against Indians and Mexicans in this part of the country. These were the days of the "red nigger" and "greaser". Many of the locals had lost friends or relatives fighting either the Indians or the Mexicans. The memory of wars can last for manny generations. Some families will never forgive. The local people would talk about the mixed race couples but as long as they stayed on their ranch they could do what they want.

Just in case of problems with his neighbors J.R. kept Molly

close to home. She didn't seem to mind. She missed her family but loved her husband. She wanted to give him many sons so he could brag around the fires of the whites. Anyway they were too busy to care what anyone else thought. J.R. was amazed at her skill with horses. He would bring in the wild horses from the open country and together they would break them. They would sell the horses and buy cattle to build a proper ranch.

A few of his Ranger friends came to the ranch to congratulate the new couple more out of curiosity than anything else. The Captain even stopped by to tell him the outcomes of their work along the Pedernales. What he really wanted to know was if J.R. was available in case he was needed. The Rangers did not like to lose men of J.R.'s knowledge of tracking and fighting the enemies of Texas. J.R. assured him that he would come when called.

The Brothers This Way Come

"Mother we brought you fresh meat. We had to ride many days but we found some deer. There are many Indians around here from all the nations, too many. They all are out hunting. The agency has not fed them as promised and their bellies are empty like ours. There are many empty bellies in this place. Many of the men are dancing the new Sun Dance and sneaking off the reservation. I think maybe there is war soon."

"Thank you my sons. You are good to take care of your poor mother living under this cloth tent with no meat to eat. You are men and must do what you think is right. Boys, I will tell you that my heart aches for your dead father. I know he rides his horse in the

Spirit World. I miss him. He made me laugh. I was proud to be his wife. He died with honor in the fight in the red canyon. What about my poor Little Mouse? Has anyone seen her? You know boys I told her that if there was ever big trouble to head for Enchanted Rock. It is many moons away. Maybe she headed for there. Boys do this one thing for me, find my sweet daughter Mouse to keep me company in my old age. Maybe she will marry a good man and they will take in an old woman. The agent here is a good man maybe if you go to him he can help you find her."

"We will try mother. We will come again and bring meat."

"Good boys."

The boys mounted their ponies and rode back to their camp in silence each lost in his own thoughts. The boys built a fire and put a hind quarter of the deer they had killed to roast. "Sun Deer, mother still believes in the agent. What lies. The whites only put us here to starve us. They want us to be red white men."

Sun Deer is by nature quiet like his sister. He follows his older brother, Big Elk. He has followed in his big brothers footsteps since they were children. He knows no other life. Big Elk and his mother are his entire world. Since moving to the reservation Sun Deer has become even more reserved and thoughtful. He only speaks to his brother when he believes it might keep them out of trouble. He knows better than try and dictate to Big Elk. "You are right brother but remember we are not looking for a fight. We are looking for our sister. We should tell the agent. He could look at the ration book names to see if Mouse is there. We can use him to help us. We also need to talk to all of the Comanche camps to see if she is there. Who knows if she is even alive. She might even be married. She was of age. Let us eat and rest and tomorrow we will look for our sister."

"Good little brother. Let us find our Mouse."

All of their efforts were in vain to find Mouse except one when they ran across one of their mother's old friends. She was sure she saw our sister and Long Walker walking toward the canyon rim when the soldiers were shooting the horses. That's all the information the brothers had about their sister when they mounted their horse, picked up their weapons and left the reservation to head back to the red canyon to search for their sister. They rode hard and fast but only at night.

"Brother we are here in the red canyon where our father and mother had put their lodge. Let us use our minds. This pile of ashes was our home. Our mother's friend lived over there. From the front of their lodges they could only see there. Do you see the canyon wall and the arroyo hidden by the brush leading to it?"

"We do not even know where the woman was when she saw our Mouse and Long Walker."

"I know but we must start somewhere. Remember Long Walker comes from the mountain horses and he always put more of his weight on his front feet. We might still find some of his tracks. If Mouse was thinking right she would leave some sign for us to follow. She might want us to find her. You start down here and I will ride to the top of the canyon and we will circle and look for her tracks. I will not go far. If either of us find the tracks bark like a fox and that will be the signal to come." It wasn't long before Sun

Deer made the sound of the fox for his brother to join him on top of the canyon. Not only had he found Long Walker tracks but also the tracks of his sister in front of the horse. There were many places where the tracks were not clear but by circling in opposite directions they would find them again."Big Elk she is heading south. She would listen to mother. Let us go to the first water south of here. This may tell us our sister's mind. You know her she was quiet but she was smart. She sure outsmarted us more than once. I don't blame her. We were mean to her many times."

"I agree brother. We will go to the springs south of here and look for tracks. If she has been there we can start to ride south at night to the next water. It is safer to travel at night. Too many enemies." They rode all day toward the hidden springs that only the Plains Indians knew the location occasionally crossing Long Walkers tracks. It was almost daylight when they approached the springs on foot. They had to be cautious in case of enemies. The springs were vacant of others so they retrieved their ponies and made camp near the springs. It was a good idea not to camp right by the water because if there were no humans present an animal might come to drink. They could use some fresh meat.

The next morning Big Elk walked to the springs to drink and there he saw his brother staring at the face of a hoodoo and smiling. "Look brother. Mother was right." There scratched into the surface of the hoodoo was a primitive drawing. "There are the signs for our father, our mother and the Spirit Rock." Now they had a destination. They would ride for the Enchanted Rock where the spirits lived. They hoped to find her near there. They searched the top of

Enchanted Rock then the Pedernales for over a week before finding where she had camped with Long Walker.

The problem was she was not alone. The other foot tracks wore moccasins but was not an Indian. Indians walk different than white men.There were another pair of shod horse tracks. She was with a white man or a Mexican. There was no signs of a fight only a camp. They would have to ride again by day to track the pair. After five days they realized the tracks were heading for Fort Sill. Maybe when they got back to the reservation Mouse would already be there with their mother. It must be a blue coat or a Ranger that found her if they were taking her back to the reservation. They talked about riding again at night since they knew her destination. Big Elk was for it but Sun Deer against it, at least until they got closer and were sure he took her there. Sun Deer was proven to be right because two days from Fort Sill the tracks turned away headed toward Texas. Why would Mouse go to Texas? She must be a slave. Caution would be needed in Texas. They had stolen many horses, taken many slaves, killed and scalped many Texans. Texans killed Comanches on sight.

So far the brothers had avoided any humans and they wanted to keep it that way. Killing would only bring trouble. They wanted no trouble unless anyone tried to stop them from retrieving their sister. Trouble was coming non the less for the pair on a ranch near Kerrville, Texas. J.R. would not let anyone relative or otherwise come between him and his new wife. He was in love and believed she felt the same about him. Love will find a way. It always does. Without love evil would conquer and their world would in deed be in chaos.

"Molly there are two Comanche braves sitting on their blankets under the big mesquite tree in front of the house. Do you know them?"

"I look. It is my brothers. They come for me. I no go. I am your wife. You are my man. Brothers mean to me. I miss mother but still no go without husband."

"You finish breakfast. Keep the rifle loaded near the stove. I will put my pistols in my belt. I will greet them as family and see what they want. If things are going well bring us coffee and breakfast. I may need you to translate. Wish me luck. If there is a fight I will need you. Here I go." J.R. walked out the door and sat down in front of the brothers. He knew better than to show any fear; before he sat he gave the signs for peace, talk and family. The rest of his conversation would be a mix of sign language and the pigeon Comanche he had learned from his wife. "Welcome my wife's brothers. We are family. Your sister is my wife."

Big Elk was the first to speak, "My sister no marry white man. Mother needs. We take her home." Both sides stared at each other in complete silence.

Sun Deer was the one to break the silence, "You bring sister. What she say?" Molly had finished cooking and was listening behind the door. Her brothers could be rude and violent. She was not sure who would win if there was an argument and a fight broke out.

"My brothers are we not men? Do we need women to speak for us? Let us relax in the shade. I promise your sister will come. She is making food with coffee and sugar." The silence was deafening. "You have ridden far. Your horses look spent. I have grain.". Again total silence.

Molly opened the door holding three cups of coffee. She kept her eyes down as she walked toward her brothers. "See brothers. My wife comes with coffee." Molly handed Big Elk a cup then Sun Deer his before serving her husband. Good manners would be important. "Drink brothers then we can talk more. See your sister. She is good with horses." Molly returned to the kitchen and came back with a big iron skillet filled with eggs, bacon biscuits and honey. She smiled at her brothers as she sat the skillet between them.

"If you need more food or coffee call me husband. My brothers are eaters," Molly let out a small laugh. This was mainly for her brothers to let them know she was happy. She hoped they got the message.

"Wife sit and join us. Maybe your brothers have news of your mother. I know from our talk you miss your mother. She taught you many things. Help me speak Comanche so me and your brothers can become friends."

"I will bring the coffee pot and sugar so you may drink your fill and then I will join you husband." Molly went inside and moved the rifle closer to the door before returning with the coffee pot and the sugar bowl. She sat by her husband keeping her eyes downcast to avoid making eye contact with her brothers. She was not completely sure how this little family gathering was going to play out.

As soon as the meal was finished J.R. spoke, "Your sister is a good wife for me. She promised me many sons. Will you bring your mother here?" This seemed to confuse the brothers. They were expecting a fight and to take Mouse home with them.

Molly sensing what was happening added to the brothers

confusion by saying, "I know husband, give my brothers three good horses to take to Mother. They can bring mother here."

Sun Deer spoke, "We are tired from our journey. We will take your horses. My brother will you let us chose the horses from your herd?"

"Yes my brother. Chose the best three." At least one of her brothers was a tricky bastard.

"We will take our horses and camp by the river not far away. We will think these things over that you have said to us," and with that the brothers cut out the three best horses and rode off towards the river.

"What do you think? Will they go or will they come back?"

"They will come back and look for a chance to talk to me with no husband or take me away by force but they will come. Maybe not tonight, maybe so. They will come."

"We will make ourselves ready for them until we know what is on their minds."

"Yes husband. We must be ready."

"You stay near the house. I'll take out the chamberpot. Only go out when you have to and carry that rifle and keep it close when you're doing chores. I have to work the livestock or they will be scattered all over the county. I'm going to move the cattle closer until this plays out."

"Be careful husband."

"Yes." J.R. not only wore his pistols he carried two extra ones on his saddle horn. Molly had the Henry rifle so he put his old Sharps in his saddle boot. He was not called the Owl for nothing.

Before he went to find his cattle he was going to find her brothers and see if he could figure out what they might be up to. He hoped and prayed he would find their trail heading for Fort Sill. He doubted it would be that easy but sometimes with Comanches it was hard to tell what was really on their minds. They could be your best friend one minute and burning you alive the next.

Once the Owl was sure the brothers were headed for the river he staked his horse and walked. He carried his Sharps in the crook of his arm. He had on his moccasins. He would walk fast and quiet through the mesquite and oak. Something was not quite right. Their trail was too easy to follow. This trail was made by comfortable people who ride among friends and are not fearful. It was obvious to him they were trying to throw him off the scent. Molly was right they would return for their sister. The next time they came to the ranch he was sure it was not to talk and drink coffee but to steal his wife one way or the other. He found them by the river, smoking and relaxing. Their five horses were hobbled near by.

Owl back tracked on his same tracks when he could, mounted his horse and went to round up his stray livestock and move them back home to graze closer to the ranch. He worked hard to be back home before dark. The night could be dangerous with two unpredictable warriors nearby. He was correct in all of his fears.

Her brothers only appeared to be negligent. They were in fact just the opposite. On one of their circular walks away from the river looking for signs of anyone coming near their camp they found her husbands moccasin tracks, the same ones from the Pederanles. They had to be their new brother-in-laws. They left a fake camp where Owl had seen them but moved themselves downriver to watch. They left their three new horses where they were but moved their mounts closer to the new camp. That night they did a reconnaissance of the house. This game of cat and mouse went on between both sides for several days. The brothers moved camp every night while they developed a plan.

Sun Deer was to approach the house of a morning to say good by to his sister and to have a smoke with his new brother-in-law before leaving. He was to say Big Elk would not come. Big Elk was angry they were leaving without their sister. Sun Deer was to assure them that he would come around given time. What Big Elk was really doing was lighting a fire behind the barn. After the fire was going good he was to move to the back of the horse corrals, remove the poles from the back, spook the horses and drive them from the corral into the grazing cattle. This would keep their brother-in-law busy. Sun Deer would grab their sister in the confusion and kick for home. Big Elk was to stay and kill their new brother-in-law and steal his horses and guns before catching the pair on the trail home.

The plan sounded good but went to shit in the execution. The grass and wood stacked behind the barn was wet from a recent heavy rain and would not light but only smoke. When Big Elk tried to remove the corral poles the horses smelled Indian and spooked before he got there. They started snorting and bucking instead of running away. The cattle meanwhile were spectators, chewing their cud and watching the show. Sun Deer kept his composure acting completely confused by all of the turmoil. When Owl ran toward the barn to investigate Sun Deer was on his feet in an instant. He ran for the house to find his sister but had to talk thru the closed door. His sister was no fool. "Mouse we have a horse for you. Big Elk waits. Let us go home to mother. You see mother then come back to husband. Mother needs you. Hurry go now or Big Elk might kill your man."

"Go away brother. This is my home with my husband. My husband is a great warrior. Big Elk may be the one to die. Go home bring my mother here. She can live with us. Go and do what men do but go!" Sun Deer turned around to see a pistol aimed at his head. He had not heard Owl walk up behind him.

"Take your brother and go. I honored my wife's family and they dishonored my home. I will not kill you as you are my wife's brother. I do not want to fight you. Go home and tell your mother to come here or we will come to the reservation to see her as soon as we can leave the ranch. I want you to take one of my wild cattle to butcher for your journey but go and go you will." Molly was aiming the Henry thru a rifle slit that had been cut in one of the boards that covered the cabin windows at Big Elk who was reaching in his quiver for an arrow to shoot his brother-in-law in the back.

She yelled at her brother, "Brother stop or I will kill you. I am not going with you. This is the end of the matter." Big Elk had notched the arrow but when he heard his sister and saw the rifle he lowered his weapon. He could kill Owl but he did not want to die today. He knew his sister well.

"We will take the cow and go. We will tell mother everything you said. Good by sister. Good by my new brother. Live in peace," with that Sun Deer walked past Owl to where his brother stood.

They walked to their horses, mounted up, gathered their cow and headed for home. At least it appeared that way. They were not satisfied with the outcome of their visit to their sister's house. The fact remained they had to return to their mother without their sister. They did not look forward to hearing the wails of their mother's sorrow. Maybe they would get lucky and her husband would die or take a white wife and throw Mouse away. Who knows. Life has no plan.

Big Elk wanted to go back right now and kill the man, burn the house, steal all the cattle and horses and make their sister go with them. She was only a woman. They had stolen many women before. She would do what she was told. Family be damned. He was a white man and manners were not important. The brothers went back to their old camp, butchered the cow and packed the meat on one of the horses Owl had given them.

While they were working they talked about what they should do. The conversation went back and forth. "Big Elk we can not kill him. He is married to our sister. He is family. Our sister is happy. She is a woman now. Mother must let her go. She is not a child anymore. They will go to mother with gifts or we can bring mother here."

"Father told us if anything happened to him we were to take care of mother. This is what we must do. The white people are why we are all starving at the agency. I hate them. The game is gone. We were free to steal, burn, fight and kill. We hunted and rode where we wanted fearing no man, Indian, Mexican or white. Now because of the whites my world is gone. I am lost brother. I am lost."

"I do not think our brother-in-law will attack us. Let us finish our work and go. I always think better when on my horse than laying around camp." They had ridden about a half day when Sun Deer turned to his brother, "We are like two waters going in opposite directions. The stronger will overcome. If neither is stronger they will stay that way forever pushing against each other and getting nowhere. Let us go to the Medicine Mounds near the Pease River. We can camp on the river, hunt for cactus medicine and go to the mounds to pray for a vision to guide us. Mother always believed in the power of the Enchanted Rock but warriors, men must go to the Medicine Mounds." That is exactly what they did.

The brothers left their horses in camp and walked to the mounds carrying neither food nor water. They had a small pouch filled with peyote cactus. They would eat nothing but this cactus for three days and nights. If they had not had a vision by then they would go home. A man needed a vision to guide him. This was the same place as young men they had prayed, fasted and received their names from the Great Spirit.

On the morning of the fourth day the two glassy eyed, hungry, thirsty, dirty brothers stared at each other without saying a word. They smiled at each other as if knowing some great secret. They hugged each other in silence, walked back to their camp, ate and drank their fill, broke camp, mounted their horses and rode back in the direction they had come. The spirits were dancing around them as they rode. This time there would be no talk. Their sister was coming home.

J.R. and Molly were exhausted from work and nerves but it seemed at last her brothers had given up and returned home. Sun

Deer must have convinced Big Elk but still in the back of her mind that little voice of doubt kept whispering in her ear, "Not so fast. Maybe they have gone, maybe not." She shared her fears with her husband. He promised to be vigilant. She knew better than to let her guard down. Only time would tell if her brothers would return. In a perfect world everyone would go home in peace. Frontier Texas was not a perfect world.

It was hard to tell what others thought no matter how close you were to them. Her brothers would do what they thought was right just like everyone else. J.R. and Molly's right thing to do was to build a ranch and a family. They had enough work for ten people. Only the idle had time to worry.

When All Else Fails Kill Them All

Big Elk could not be killed in battle against the whites. In his vision the cactus rose from the desert floor and whispered in his ear that he was invincible in war against them. In Sun Deer's vision he was walking in the desert and he saw his brother in the distance. His brother began to glow as if on fire. He knew his brother was blessed by the Great Spirit and he would follow him anywhere. They were going to get their sister and take her to their mother. They were now fearless men who would create havoc on their journey. They rode straight and hard toward Kerrville throwing caution to the wind. They would hide no more.

The first ranch they came to they made no plan, had no discussion. They went straight to a white woman working in her garden. Big Elk raped her then scalped her before chopping off her hands with an axe that had been lying nearby. He thought it was funny the way she tried to pull herself along by her bleeding stumps where her hands had been. When she tried to rise he chopped off her feet. She would die soon enough. There had been a baby sleeping that had woke up from the screams of his mother. Big Elk bashed its head against a stone. Sun Deer walked into the house and found a Henry rifle and a box of bullets. He let out a war whoop of victory before lighting the house on fire from the hot coals still glowing in the fireplace. Big Elk tied the woman's scalp to his war bridle. It was the first of many. They walked over to the corral before leaving and shot all of the horses, cows, and goats. This was a trick they had learned from the blue coats at the fight in the red canyon.

The next killing was two Mexican vaqueros working cattle. Big Elk left with two black scalps added to his bridle. They added three pistols and two more rifles to their arsenal. They shot the Mexicans in the back with arrows. They had not known the brothers were there. One of the Mexicans tried to race away on his horse. Sun Deer shot him with his new rifle. He didn't care for scalps so he let his brother take this one. That was the lucky Mexican. The other vaquero had fallen off of his horse. He tried to run so Big Elk shot him in the left hamstring. When the vaquero tried to hop away on one leg Big Elk shot him in the other hamstring. The Mexican fell to the ground and tried to reach for his pistol. Big Elk pinned the man's forearm to the ground with another arrow. The wounded Mexican dropped the pistol and could no longer pick it up. Big Elk walked over and scalped the man while still alive. He then tore open the man's shirt and skinned his back. The man would not stop screaming. At first the Indian thought it was funny but then it became annoying. He turned the man over and stabbed him in the heart with his knife.

Two days later another white ranch was burning. Burning in the yard were the family: a man, his wife and their three children. All had been scalped and tortured before being placed on the coals from their burning house. The wife had been raped along with a teenage daughter. The women had their privates removed to make pouches to carry peyote or tobacco. The man and boys had been castrated and their privates shoved in their mouths. Big Elk only added the scalps of the adults to his bridle. There was no honor in the scalps of children. He only scalped the children because he felt like it at the time. They again shot all of the livestock except taking two horses to help carry the guns and supplies they had stolen.

The boys continued this reign of terror all the way to Kerrville. By the end of the second week there was a posse of Texas Rangers on their trail. For these Indians the guilty verdict was in and they would be killed as soon as they could be found. The brothers knew eventually the whites would seek vengeance but they did not care. Big Elk was a holy warrior. Let them try and kill him.

They rode straight to their sister's house. She was inside preparing the evening meal. Owl was nowhere to be seen. Unknown to the brothers he was only a few yards away in the outhouse. J..R. heard riders in his yard and peeked out of a crack in the wooden door. It was her brothers. He noticed the fresh scalps hanging from Big Elk's bridle. J.R. picked his pistols up from the outhouse floor because his pants were around his ankles while he was taking a dump. He pushed open the door with his feet and shot Big Elk as he walked toward the house. He shot him again to be sure he was down. Sun Deer raised his rifle and pointed toward the outhouse but before he could shoot his sister shot him from the front door. He fell over dead. Big Elk was still moaning so J.R. shot him a third time. this time in the back of the head.

They buried them both in a plot behind the barn. A few days later the Texas Rangers rode into the ranch after trailing them there. J.R. told them the story and showed them the graves. One of the rangers spit on the grave. One rancher whose relatives had been killed pissed on the grave. Molly came out to bring them coffee.. As soon as the rangers saw her they went back to the graves and dug them up to be sure they were in there just in case J.R. had turned into an Indian lover and were hiding them. The rangers saw the scalps taken from Big Elk's horse as further proof. They buried the scalps in a separate grave away from the graves of the Indians. A few days later Molly asked J.R. to write a letter to the agent at Fort Sill explaining what happened to her brothers, asking if he would please tell her mother. She had him add that she and her husband would come in the spring to fetch her mother back to the ranch with them. This would not happen. Two days after Christmas Molly received a letter from the agency that her mother had died of pneumonia due to a very cold and wet winter.

Molly wanted children now more than ever. She was now the last of her family. They were trying to have children even though they were still exhausted every day of their lives from their work building their ranch. Their life was work. Molly and J.R. were both still young. Molly was still a teenager, J.R, in his twenties. Children would come but not just yet.

The Governor Needs a Bodyguard

Reconstruction. Hah! Guerilla War was more like it: old animosities among the whites and the Mexicans, Mexican feuds, white feuds, carpetbaggers, political foes, bandits, rustlers, whiskey and gun runners, smugglers of every description on the coast and the border, renegade Indians from the nations, no money, no jobs, the economy destroyed, a lost war, the free black soldiers running loose, the KKK. The governor had decided it was time for him to call for help. The U.S. Army had proved to be more of a problem then a solution. He was desperate to regain control of a state that was rapidly approaching total anarchy. He recalled the best and most loyal proven fighters in the state, the Texas Rangers. What he wanted was an elite police force to enforce the Radical Republican agenda being forced on the state from Washington. What he got was one company of exRangers that believed in the future of Texas, not politics.

Governor Andrew Jackson Hamilton who had been appointed military governor by Lincoln during the war was now the appointed provincial governor. He had attempted an armed coup in Texas during the war which had ended in failure. He was a political appointee and not a popular choice among the people of Texas. He was there to make sure Reconstruction was enforced and the state was cleared from the control of powerful Democrat insurrectionist. The straw that broke the camel's back was the assassination attempt on him that by the Grace of God and a paid informant had failed.

The call for the Rangers to assemble went out across the state. When enough men had assembled a former Captain in the Rangers was promoted to Major and told to form a company and their assignment was to protect Austin, the surrounding country side and most importantly to protect the life of the Governor. If he could stay alive in these troubled times this force of exRangers would at least provide the illusion that the state was under some order until he could buy enough time to overcome his enemies and all of the violence and theft descending on the state. He wanted a personal bodyguard he could trust with his life. What he got was, J.R. Grinder.

"Mr. Grinder I am told you are a man of grit and determination. There has been at least one attempt on my life. I need a personal bodyguard that will be vigilant in his duties. Texas is in a crucial point in her history."

"I was called up. The Major said I was to report to you. If that is what you need for me to do then I will do it."

"I do not know where your sympathies were in the war but I was assured you are a loyal man. Do you mind if I ask you a personal question?" Without waiting for an answer, "Is it true that you shot both of your brothers-in-law?"

"My sympathies as you call them are for Texas. The other question is private family business."

"You get settled in the Congress Hotel then report back here. The state is paying for your room and board."

"If I'm to stay in Austin I'm bringing my wife here. She won't be safe out on the ranch by herself."

"That is your business. Feel free to put her up in the hotel when she arrives."

"I'm leaving today to go get her. Be back in a week."

"I need a bodyguard now Mr. Grinder."

"Then get yourself one," and with that J.R. turned and walked out of the Governor's office, mounted his pony and headed for Kerrville.

No Comanche Wanted Here

True to his word J.R. returned with Molly riding Long Walker by his side in one week. They rode straight to the Congress Hotel and tied their ponies out front. Both of them grabbed their bedrolls and saddlebags and walked toward the stairs to go to J.R.'s room. The clerk behind the desk when he saw the couple stopped what he was doing and yelled across the room, "Just a minute sir. Where are you going?"

"I'm going to my room."

"We have a no Indian policy here. You can't take that woman with you."

"The woman is my wife and she goes where I go."

"I'm sorry sir but not here. You will have to find other lodging." J.R. stopped, turned and stared at the man. The lobby had become deadly quiet as other guest waited in silence for the drama to play itself out.

"Come on Molly let's go find a place to camp." J.R. knew as soon as he said it that camping with Molly near Austin was a bad idea. He would not be able to leave her alone. She

35

was brave and tough that was for sure but if evil men wanted to cause her trouble they would. J.R. went straight to the Major and told him about the problem he had at the hotel.

"It' ll be that way all over town here J.R. These folks here still remember the Council House fight and don't like Indians much. I think they hate about everybody they didn't grow up with. They hate Yankees, Mexicans, Niggers and Indians and not necessarily in that order. Too many bad feelings, Too much bad history. I tell you what. Me and the Mrs. have a ranch south of town.

You all head for Spicewood Springs and right before you get there you'll see a well used cow path with some buggy ruts headed east. Follow the buggy ruts that until you get to the ranch house. We will like the company. After you get the Mrs. settled report back to the governor."

"Reckon he still wants me to bodyguard?"

"He wants you alright. He told me about you walking out. He was fit to be tied. I thought it was funny as hell. He needs us. I know it and he knows it. Besides he couldn't find a better man if he tried. I'll see you later at the ranch," and with that J.R. took Molly to their new temporary home in the woods near Spicewood. It turned out to be a piece of heaven on earth. They both helped around the ranch and all four became good friends for the rest of their lives.

One year later as soon as the governor departed for a new government job in New Orleans, J.R. retired from the Rangers this time for good. He and Molly returned home to what was left of their ranch they had spent their lives struggling to build. It was a mess. The house and barn had literally been stolen; both had been stripped of lumber and rock to the point there was hardly anything left but a lone chimney. The corral was broken down and the outhouse had been turned over. The only building left standing was the rock spring house. The well house minus the roof was there and the water was still good. What was left of the cattle were scattered to kingdom come, the few that had not been stolen. Welcome Home!

What the couple did was make a camp and get to work. They had J.R.'s Ranger wages and the money they had buried before leaving. No use in complaining or being vengeful. It was a waste of time. They got themselves lost in the business of rebuilding their home and starting a family. They would be blessed with both, a working horse and cattle ranch to be proud of and a huge family to help work it. They would be blessed with six children, four boys and two girls. All would be raised to be ranchers, to be true sons and daughters of Texas.

Aftermath

War, the ultimate human folly or the natural consequence of the tribal nature for conquest, who knows! Whatever causes war for those that survive the memories run deep. Generations later after the popular press and entertainments have migrated on, the stories of a war will be retold around the dinner table for many generations. Atrocities are not easily forgotten. Families don't forget predators that brutalized their ancestors. This is human nature..

In Texas it is still true today from survivors of the Indian Wars, the war with Mexico and the Civil War. The young people think it is all folly but the old know that history has a way of repeating itself. The scars of war run deep. It was not until 1980 that the descendants of the Crider family convinced the State of Texas and the Texas Rangers to recognize the graves of J.P. Crider and his Comanche wife Polina. Maybe memories do have an expiration date! This is only one of the many truer than fiction stories about Texas, the real Texas born of blood, sweat, tears and yes, love.

The End

The Confession

After what I did at work today I know you will come straight here to my home. I am either dead or in jail. In case I am dead I thought I should let you know who you had killed. You thought I was a nothing, a non entity. Read my confession and you will see how wrong you all are.

I killed my first victim when I was ten. I was walking home from school and the drainage ditch near my house was running deep and strong from the recent storms. I saw a kid from school hanging for dear life to a clump of grass. He had fallen in and by the look on his face was too terrified to scream. At first I tried to help him get out but he made no effort to help himself so I stomped on his hands until he let go. I watched the swift running water wash him away. He went a little ways before disappearing for good under the water.. I didn't feel anything and I didn't say a word to anybody. His disappearance was a big deal around town for a while. They finally found his body in the swamp.The verdict was accidental drowning. Too easy!

The next kid I killed I was fifteen. His older brother had bullied me for years. I caught his little brother walking home alone from a Friday night little league game. I hit him from behind right square in the head with a large rock. He fell down. I had never seen so much blood. He didn't scream or anything just laid there and bled. I stood there just watching the blood rushing out. I didn't know the human body had so much blood. Later on when the whole town was looking for a child killer mom said the dead kid had been a hemophiliac and couldn't stop bleeding. I had never heard that word before, hemophiliac. No wonder there was so much blood. Tough shit!

By the time I was seventeen I was bored with small town life so I quit school and hitchhiked to the big city to make my way. I slept in parks, stole and panhandled for a while until I found a job in a warehouse loading trucks. I only killed one person while I was living in the parks, a teenage girl that had run away from home and was living like me. I strangled her in a drainage culvert where she was sleeping. I remember jerking off later that night. I never heard if they found her body or not. Who cares!

I was too busy working and putting a life together for the next few years to hurt anyone. One of the guys at work taught me to drive a truck. I got promoted to driving. I drove only local deliveries at first. In two years I had graduated to driving the big rigs across country. That's when I got busy. Truck driving can be really boring and lonely.

I killed mostly queers and run aways. Fun! I did do a couple of really pretty women that had broken down on the interstate. Both were late at night when the interstate was quiet. I bashed in one''s head with a tire iron. The other one was so terrified I put her in the truck and made her give me a blow job then I raped her front and back before I strangled her. I left both bodies in the car. That was a close one I thought I was caught for sure more than once. Easy does it cowboy!

After that I cooled it for awhile but fate has a way of intervening doesn't it. A couple of the boys were smuggling drugs for the cartels and introduced me to Juan. I ran dope for the cartel for three years before Juan approached me about a way to make some extra money, good money. They needed a rival killed and wanted to know if I was interested. Was I interested? Hell, yes. I got a hard on just listening to Juan. I told Juan to give me a picture of the guy and where he lived and I would take care of the rest. Two days later there was a manila envelope lying on my driver's seat, inside was all the info I needed to find one, Jorge Rivera, age forty-two living the quiet life in the suburbs. There was also a cell phone number with the drawing of a scorpion underneath. The scorpion was the symbol of Juan's cartel. It was on all of the packages of cocaine I had smuggled in my truck. I was off and running for my new career that would last for years.

Jorge Rivera was a different ball game for me. He was a professional criminal and cartel associate. I always loved hunting shows on tv and gangster movies. Believe it or not this is where I learned my trade. I stalked Jorge for two weeks before establishing a pattern, if you could call it a pattern. Jorge was a careful man. When I had my plan formulated I called the cell number and requested a pistol and a silencer. Two days later there was a gift wrapped box on the seat of my truck, inside was a .40 caliber Glock equipped with a silencer.

Every morning after getting the kids off to school Jorge and his wife, still in their bathrobes enjoyed a morning coffee and orange juice while reading their mail from the day before and the morning papers. Routine is what a professional killer looks for. I also knew from my observations that the driveway was blocked from view by the front door. They had cameras on their doorbell so that presented a problem. I bought myself a post office uniform, a mail bag, a wig, beard and mustache, dark glasses and a post office cap. I planned on keeping my head low as I spoke into the doorbell camera.

Ding, dong. "Can I help you?"

"Mr. Rivera I have a package here from Mexico that must be signed for. I could not leave it in your mail box yesterday."

"OK, Pass it thru the crack in the door will you I'm not dressed?"

"I would sir but the package will not fit. Would you please open the door so I can get this done. I have a lot of deliveries today. I would like to get on my way."

"Just leave it on the porch."

"I can't do that sir. It would be my job. I will have to return the package to the post office and you will have to retrieve it there. Thank you," and with that I turned around to leave. It didn't matter either way. If this didn't work I would pop him somewhere else.

"Ok, Ok, just a minute." When the chain was removed and the door was starting to be pushed open, I pulled the Glock from my mailbag, while kicking the door into his face.

"God da......," was all he got out before I shot him twice. A pistol lay on the floor that either had fallen out of his pocket or his hand. I ran the three steps to the dining room table where his wife was in the process of standing up, the look of absolute horror on her face. She like her husband knew death would eventually come just not now. I shot her twice before walking over and putting one in her face. On the way out I put one more in Jorge's face just to make sure. I walked out the door, got in my stolen car with fake government plates and went to dispose of everything I had used. I threw the pistol and silencer into the Mississippi River while crossing the bridge. Everything else I burned in the car after removing the plates. Five gallons of gasoline will eliminate any over sites on my part. I shredded the plates before disposing of the pieces in gas stations scattered over the the city.

The bodies weren't discovered until the children returned from school that day. No one had seen anything, at least that was what the papers said. Juan was happy. I found an envelope stuffed with cash on my kitchen table. I'm sure this method of delivery was chosen to let me know they could get to me anytime. I would have to learn to be prey and predator at the same time. Now at last I had a job where I could earn some real money and at the same time enjoy my work. It is a rare thing in this world for a man to find joy in his work.

Between my paychecks from driving, smuggling drugs and as a hit man I was living good, modestly but good. I believed in saving money not blowing it on things you don't need. The world does turn and circumstances can always change. It was not a good idea to bring too much attention to yourself in my kind of work, not only from your enemies but also your bosses if they became too paranoid.

My next job would be harder than the first or so I thought.

This job was for a woman. A wealthy woman complete with body-guards. Her bodyguards turned out to be her weakness. She was over confident in her bodyguards abilities plus the fact she was fucking one of them helped. She was so hot for this guy she would even fuck him in the back of her limo. I just had to bide my time. She was a bit of a wild one having been raised a spoiled brat from a rich family and liked to take chances. I had no idea what she had done to piss my bosses off but it usually involved money. Rich kids like to play tough at least until tough plays back. It would cost this one her life. She was fucking her bodyguard in her limo in an alley outside of a club in New York. I opened the back door and emptied a silenced Uzi into the pair. I left the untraceable gun there, walked to the subway and disappeared. I went to my hotel, ordered two es-corts and expressed my happiness in sex. Life was good was it not.

I needed a challenge. I really wanted to be a real gangster in-stead of just a trigger man. I chopped up my next bodies out of frus-tration. What could I do to become a real gangster? This was really working on my mind. I didn't want to wait for another job. Killing relaxes me and helps me to think. I needed to practice my trade.

I like to think that I'm not a bad looking man. One of my char-acters I like to play was "good old boy", complete with pickup truck. "Good old boy" picked up a waitress from a restaurant out on a quiet county road. I promised if she would go with me I would take her to the big city and show her a good time. I played drunk while she got shit faced. I drove her out in the country to an aban-doned house. I pulled my car into the garage. So far so good. After we screwed and swore we were in love I asked her if it wouldn't be fun to explore the old house. At first she didn't want anything to do with the creepy place but eventually she gave in. I had scouted out the old house weeks before and had all of my tools inside. When she looked in the bathroom door I stabbed her in the neck and threw her in the bathtub. She was still breathing and garbling so I cut her throat. I took my saw and just like in the movies I cut her into six pieces. What a fucking mess! I forgot the water wasn't on. I put the six pieces in black garbage bags carried them out to the garage where I had an empty barrel to put her in. I put the barrel in the back of the truck, filled the barrel with rocks and sealed it. I lit the house on fire. Fire has a cleansing property that can't be beat.

I then drove to a lake nearby, backed as close as I could to the water, opened the tailgate and rolled the barrel into the water. I sweated over that one for years afraid that I had left too many clues and would be caught. I had left witnesses at the cafe. What if the barrel was found and she was identified! After a while I just quit worrying. Worry does nothing but add feelings of guilt. Fuck guilt. I was having fun.

My next job for Juan was one of my proudest moments. I did it just like in the movie,"The Godfather." I walked into a restaurant, relaxed, had a meal, pretended to look on my phone for a while, got up and walked to the bathroom. I walked out not looking at anyone as I headed for my table. Right before I got to my table I detoured one step to the right, pulled a twenty-two that had electric tape on the handle and trigger. I had wiped the gun clean beforehand and had on a pair of lambskin gloves. I shot the man five times in the back of the head and dropped the gun there. I wasn't worried about physical evidence. I had cased the place a favorite hangout of the victim and it was old school, home cooking and most importantly no cameras. My only worry was eye witnesses. I had dyed my hair, put on a fake mustache and used theatrical makeup to make my skin darker with a big scar on one cheek. I knew I was taking chances but it aroused me to push the limits. After burning my clothes and makeup I went to a porno theater where I got a blow job from a faggot. I lured him outside with the promise of a drink and a room. I strangled him with my belt and left his body in a dumpster in the alley. Fucking pervert.

Juan or somebody that worked for him was leaving bigger and bigger envelopes. The world was good. I treated myself to a vacation where I strangled a little girl I found alone on the beach. I rented a boat and threw her in the ocean. I really got pissed at myself for working while on vacation. What kind of parent loses track of a child at night on a beach! What a couple of assholes! They deserve whatever they get. I bet they won't make that mistake again.

When I had enough money hidden I disappeared. I left no trace for Juan to find me. I have a new name, new town and a new beginning. I found a woman who loved me and started a family. I found a job as far from my old one as possible. A good citizen must have a job, a family and show a way to support them. That is me good neighbor Sam.

"Samual come to dinner it's getting cold. You better go to bed early tonight. You know you have to get to school early tomorrow to wax the gym floor before the pep rally."

"Yes dear, Just a minute."

I need to finish now. I can no longer live with my memories from my past and the slow death of my present. The authorities will now have my confession to prove I am not a nobody like my wife and kids think I am. No boss or teacher or spoiled kid will ever tell me what to do or make fun of me again. My children will no longer lower their eyes in shame when they see me at work. My wife and children I will kill today out of mercy the others would be just in the wrong place at the wrong time and mean nothing to me, no more than swatting flies. Fuck 'em. Goodby. Samual Jones.

Samuel Jones was correct on where the police would go after the massacre. The police after one of the most brutal murders in the state of California and the nation as a whole went to the home of Samuel Jones, custodian where they found the bodies of his wife and children and his so called confession. His total body count for the day was twenty-three with several more wounded taken to the hospital. The police killed Samuel Jones as he was attempting to reload his AK-47. Later the gymnasium where the brutal attack had taken place at the Beverly Hills High School pep rally would be torn down and replaced. After an intense police investigation Samuel Jones seemed to appear out of thin air, a man with no past; and to this day his confession could neither be proven or disproven.

The End

The Tunnels
of Chu Chi

Taste Test

B urton Coffee Travis III, known to his friends as B.C. considered himself a connoisseur of dust. He claimed due to the frequent dust storms in West Texas to have swallowed and breathed in at least one pound of dust from his home in Midland County, Texas, as well as a pound each from the surrounding counties and maybe with a strong enough westerly wind the occasional hint of the taste of Eastern New Mexico. He claimed that if were given a spoonful of dirt from any county in West Texas with one taste or snort he could tell you what county it came from. He swore he could tell Midland County dirt by only sniffing the spoon as Midland County had the added scent of bullshit. You might have to have lived in West Texas to get the joke but he didn't care. He repeated anyway and often to his buddies at the Army's 25th Division Combat Base in Cu Chi, Republic of Vietnam.

During the dry season the red dust of Vietnam was often the subject of conversation during the down times between operations. B.C. argued the dust here was indeed different than that of West Texas, more of a clay base than sand. It was so thick here at times you could slice it with a knife. The morning air could be red, purple, green or yellow as you walked thru it around the base. The damn red dirt got into everything and if allowed to get wet could get as hard as cement. B.C. in his morning ritual walk to the outhouse sniffed the early morning air and decided the dirt of Vietnam tasted somewhere between diesel, insecticide, tear gas, gunpowder and a urinal that had never been cleaned. He by far preferred the taste of good old West Texas dirt.

B.C. had reenlisted this time for one reason only. The promise to get him out of his LRRP, (Long Range Reconnaissance Patrol), platoon and make him a Tunnel Rat. He had found a home and a value to his life in the Army. His new life beat the hell out of what his future would have been in the oil fields of West Texas. He liked hunting men. It was a challenge because these bastards were hunting you, too. The adrenalin rush from combat was addictive. He knew that he could find the bastards in the jungle. He fine tuned his senses to the point he was about half blood hound and half seeing eye dog. When going to the field he had stopped using anything that might dull his senses or carry an odor to the enemy: booze, drugs, cigarettes, chewing gum, soap, deodorant. These habits would come in handy and would reenforce his presence in his new job in the tunnels of Chu Chi and the Iron Triangle.

He wondered what it would be like to get up close and personal in the tunnels with one of his little brown brothers; to look him in the eyes and feel his breath on you as you killed the cocksucker. He would enter a tunnel with only a pistol, flashlight and a knife. Later as the size and complexity of the tunnels became known a rope would be tied to him so he could find his way back in the dark, the darkness of the grave.

B.C. had killed plenty of gooks with his rifle and grenades. A new perspective of life had changed him from his initial fear of combat to a grim determination to survive. He felt nothing staring at the bodies of his dead enemies. He was not without feeling or compassion, missing only his friends that had been wounded or killed and shipped out. He tried not to get too close to anyone except the fully committed to their task at hand. The rotation system was so fucked up that by the time you got to know a guy and he got good at his job the fucker was gone or was dead.

He didn't consider himself brave, on his first combat operation he had had plenty of fear, in fact he was scared shitless. The first time his sergeant told him to shoot into the jungle he forgot to release the safety on his M-14. He hadn't seen anyone to shoot at and just kept firing into the jungle until he was told to stop. His wakeup call came when a sniper's shot buzzed inches from his head as it passed to kill the man behind him.

His first impulse had been to go straight for the ground; as he lay there he talked himself into getting control of his nerves and his fears. Watching the blood pouring out of the man's head lying next to him he decided right then and there it was better for his enemy to fear him than the other way around; in every firefight from then on he was calm and in control of himself. A man who could control himself in dangerous situations was a man to fear. He taught himself to be as calm as possible no matter what happened in the field.

As long as he concentrated what was going on around him and kept his focus he had no time for fear. Fear was death. He had pushed his fears deep in his psyche.

B.C. convinced himself that the saying, "if a man says he was not scared he was a liar", was bullshit. Maybe he was a broken unit. God had simply removed fear as a part of his personality. He wasn't a bragger or a risk taker. He became a man that was very methodical. He enjoyed his work. He thought of himself as a skilled professional whose tool was a gun. His job was to find Communist and kill them. That is why he was a perfect fit for the LRRP's and now for the Tunnel Rats.

Like the LRRPS the Tunnels Rats were elite, a brotherhood of fearless and crazy bastards doing a job nobody else would do. They would do anything for each other: lie, cheat, steal, kill. B.C.'s reputation had proceeded him. The Captain gave him the best of the best to teach him the ropes of the job. His teacher was a rabid anti-Communist who had fought against Castro in Cuba, Jorge Ramon.

As soon as Jorge escaped Cuba for the U.S. he joined the Army, asked for combat and Vietnam. They gave him both. He liked killing Communist. He had a lot of scores to settle. Fidel proved to be a megalomaniac bullshitter. He grabbed power, promoted his friends then began a campaign to rid Cuba of her enemies as defined by Fidel. A lot of people died and were robbed to keep Fidel in houses, yachts and wives. Fucking Communist. Share the wealth my ass. America has it right: do your best, earn your way and move on. He fucking loved America.

Ho, Ho, Ho

Ho Duc Loc was alone now. His family had been killed in the latest American bombing of Hanoi. His family had been evaporated by a direct hit from a 500 lb. bomb. Ho was in shock.

He had been at work when the air raid struck. He was a construction worker who had helped to build the individual bomb shelters that were scattered along the streets of the city. The current project he had been employed to do was a large bomb shelter complex directly under the city hospital. Ho had been lucky he was in the shelter during the attack; then he walked home.

Ho stared into the bomb crater that had once been his home and swore vengeance against the Americans. They were murderers and he would get even if it was the last thing he would do. His only possessions were the clothes on his back and a wallet where he carried the pictures of his dead wife and children. His family was gone, disappeared. He didn't even have a body to bury. He sat by the crater the rest of the day crying and praying.

The next morning Ho joined the North Vietnamese Army. He was sent to Cambodia near the South Vietnamese border to help repair the Ho Chi Minch trail against the continuous bombing assaults of the Americans. Ho was a skilled worker and was soon given authority over the civilians working alongside the soldiers. He worked harder than he ever had in his life with a grim determination driving him on to try and get closer to the Americans. He wanted more than anything to trade his pick and his basket for a gun. He wanted to fight and kill Americans. His officers admired his spirit and if he would be patient and do his duty to Uncle Ho and his country they promised he would soon get his chance. As the repair work on the trail was turned over to the civilian laborers Ho Duc Loc was reassigned to build tunnels for the Viet Cong. His next job would be in South Vietnam near the town of Chu Chi.

Here Ho got his wish. He was trained to be a proper soldier. He was taught how to shoot and keep an AK47 clean and operable, to throw grenades and kill with a knife. Ho was taught to obey orders in indoctrination classes. He was taught about how Communism was the salvation of his country from the Imperialist who only cared about conquest and the subjugation of Vietnam. He was taught his country was one country, not two separate countries but one, one country, one people, one government and that government would be Communist. His leaders taught him that the government of South Vietnam were only American puppets and did not care for the people of Vietnam only its wealth. He was shown videos of dogs attacking blacks somewhere in America. He was told this was what would happen to the Vietnamese if the Americans won the war. Now more than ever Ho wanted to punish the Americans and the traitors in the South Vietnamese Army. He wanted to use his new skills to kill them.

Ho Duc Loc was assigned to the 9th Division of the People's Army of North Vietnam. He joined his unit in what the Americans called the Iron Triangle near Cu Chi in South Vietnam. Ho's first job was guard duty for the propaganda and tax collection officers who snuck into the local villages at night; in this capacity he was told to avoid the Americans. He wanted to fight, this duty would not do. Be patient he was told. The Americans aren't stupid and will soon show up at night and you can kill as many as you like.

Ho had no way of knowing it but his 9th Division were about to be committed along with the 7th NVA Division to digging a complete division headquarters right under the feet of the Americans. He was told he was a soldier now and must do his duty whatever it was. Do what you are told for our final victory. Dig for the revenge of your murdered family. A soldier that does not do his duty would be punished. Vietnam had no room for halfway patriots. Ho got the message and put his nose to the grindstone. He might be digging tunnels but he would keep his AK47 clean and ready. He knew he would eventually get his chance. His chance was called Tet.

They ran out of their tunnels for the city of Saigon and the large airbase at Ton Son Nhut. Each soldier was assigned a team with a specific task: murder, kidnapping, destruction, confusion, propaganda. Ho Chi Minh was convinced if he attacked the major urban centers in force the South Vietnamese people would rally to his cause to cast out the Americans. Bad guess Ho! The South Vietnamese loved the Americans and their endless wealth. They wanted to live like the Americans not the peasants of Communism.

The fight was on, it would be brutal and long with the Americans winning and driving the NVA and Viet Cong back to their tunnels and bases in the jungles. The Americans won the fight but NVA propaganda officers told them not to worry. The Americans might win a fight but Uncle Ho Chi Minh promised them they would not lose the war. One battle is not the war! War is a living, breathing organism with many interlinking components; when all is in unison victory will be ours. Have faith bothers and sisters.

Ho Duc Loc survived the battle. He had been in one of the squads that had attacked the airbase to blow up airplanes, kill Americans and create confusion. Most of his unit was killed but Ho had managed to fight his way back to the tunnels. His blood lust had still not been satisfied. He had shot at Americans but wasn't sure he had hit any.

The Americans were completely surprised. There was no way that many men could be hidden in the jungle without being found. After the fight was over the Americans began to realize the scale of the tunnel complexes that must be around the South for this many enemies to appear as ghost out of nowhere. Nowhere turned out to be a smuggling route that included a tunnel complex soon to be 200 kms long coming from the Cambodia border at the nexus of the Ho Chi Minh trail then following the Saigon River to the Iron Triangle and further south toward the city of Chu Chi complete with at least three NVA headquarters. The American knew there was no mystery to the problem of the ghost soldiers. If they were not in the jungle they had to be under it. During the war with France the guerrillas had been industrious in the building of tunnels to attack the French. There had to be vast underground works somewhere and the Americans were determined to find them.

The Americans found some of the tunnels they were looking for under their feet when they unknowingly built the 25th Division Headquarters right on top of a major complex. This has to be the very definition of the word irony. The enemy were attacking them from inside their own lines until they eventually figured out where the ambushes were coming from. Surprise! What fucking nerve!

When Ho was not digging he was busy setting up ambushes near tunnel entrances. As the Americans became more than ever determined to destroy the tunnels surrounding their base with floods, gas and explosions Ho became a driving force in the sophistication of the tunnel complex. He supervised the digging of levels and put in doors to control floods and gases. Because of the nature of the clay soil small plastic explosives were not a huge concern. All you had to do was dig to repair the damage. He made sure the ventilation and smoke holes worked with the winds and vegetation. His personal favorite idea was the false tunnels to lead the Americans on dead ends equipped with death traps of all description: poisonous snakes tied to stakes, poison punji sticks under vegetation, trip grenades or men like Ho waiting with a knife and a gun.

Ho's commanders liked one of his ideas so much they rewarded Ho's ingenuity with a week leave to Saigon complete with gold coins to spend as he liked for his unique idea of reconstructing the bomb shelters in the shape of triangles to deflect bomb blast. These shelters were so acoustically designed approaching bombers could be heard getting close before the actual raid could take place. Ho walked the streets of Saigon, drank Tiger beer and watched the Americans. He thought his fellow countrymen in the South were no more than beggars, thieves and whores. It was the Americans he studied as a tiger studies a herd of water buffalo. Ho was expanding his hunting skills.

The Eyes Have It

B.C. learned his craft well from Jorge. They became an inseparable pair. After blowing up a hospital complex with 300 lbs of C-4 the NVA put a bounty on both of their heads. They were put on the top ten hit list of the NVA. This was considered a badge of honor by the pair. Some of their buddies made up wanted posters like you would see in an American western tv programs, complete with pictures and bounties. They hung them around the base.

Ho wasn't laughing and he didn't care about the reward. He was angry because the hospital had been his work. Ho took this disaster to the tunnels personally. He had worked in the hospital in Hanoi and wanted more than anything to help his wounded comrades. His commanders had their agents steal copies of the fake reward posters from inside the American base at Chu Chi. They showed these posters to Ho and told him these were the men responsible for destroying his work. They came into the tunnels often. They gave Ho the job of finding these men and killing them before they could do more damage. They knew he was the right man for the job.

Jorge went into the tunnel like he had one hundred other times. After letting out fifty yards of rope Jorge tugged three times waited then tugged three more times this was the signal for found something big. Immediately the rope went slack. Too much time had passed and there were no other messages coming from Jorge's rope. B.C. knew as soon as he pulled on the rope that Jorge was not attached to the other end. Had he taken it off to maneuver in a tight space like he had so many times before? Maybe he was exploring on his own. He had signaled he had found something big. He might be lying quietly to avoid detection. Up here on the surface there was no way to know. God forbid something had happened to him! "Patience, B.C. patience", was what B.C. kept telling himself. The rule was after a disconnect as soon as possible the Rat in the tunnel was to pull one time wait and pull twice that was signal for going solo. The rope remained slack. "Fuck it. I'm going in."

What Jorge found was Ho. Jorge sniffed the air. He studied the ground in front of him longer than he normally did. Something was not right. Jorge cut off his flashlight, sat on the tunnel floor, fined tuned his senses and waited. He was detecting nothing, no sound, no smell, no tracks, only the darkness of the grave. As soon as he felt safe to do so Jorge gently dropped on his hands and knees and silently crawled forward, one step. He heard the rope drag behind him, cursed to himself, unsnapped the rope from his belt, signaled to B.C. that he had found something big after seeing the headquarters sign and waited again for all of his senses to go back on overdrive; as soon as he felt it was safe he moved forward once again. There it was. He was sure this time, the slightest hint of garlic. There was the silence of the tomb as Ho emerged from his well concealed hole he had dug into the side wall of the fake tunnel.

Ho was proud of his deceptions. He had placed signs pointing to a dead end tunnel as if it led to their headquarters. Ho had rubbed garlic on the tunnel walls in exactly the place he wanted the American to stop. Ho fired three rounds from his AK47 into the tight space of the tunnel. The light from the muzzle flash showed the face of a shocked American wearing no shirt and carrying a pistol. Jorge was dead.

B.C. followed the rope alternately looking with the flashlight and in the dark as he thought the situation demanded. B.C. found the end of the rope, a blood pool and nothing else. B.C. as quiet as he could despite the fact he felt as if his beating heart could be heard outside of his body moved cautiously until he found the headquarters sign, the end of the dummy tunnel and the hole built into the side. There was no body to be found.

Impossible, B.C. had overlooked something. Men just don't disappear. It had definitely been a well planned trap. He had to be careful or he would be next. B.C. would search for his friend until he found him or was killed himself. B.C. was not scared of death. He had seen plenty of it by now. He did not seek death but if it came, what the fuck. You wouldn't know a damn thing about it. You were just gone that was all.

What Ho had done was use a secret trap door to the surface to remove both himself and the body of Jorge. Ho stripped the body of Jorge, cut off his penis and balls and shoved them in his mouth. He took the fake wanted poster of Jorge and stuck it to his chest with Jorge's own knife. He then tied the body to a tree near the tunnel entrance to be sure it would be found.

As soon as B.C. emerged from the tunnel and saw what was left of his friend he transcended. For those that have ever experienced this in combat you know you are no longer a man but an animal. The eyes become glazed over, Others are speaking but you do not hear. Conversation is over, orders are over. B.C. picked up his gear and walked over to the tree where his friend had been tied and he sat down and he waited. Dark was coming and the men he was working with returned to the pickup point to be taken to camp. They carried the body of Jorge. B.C. sat under the tree waiting for the darkness and the enemy that would come.

One American bastard killed and one to go. The first trap had worked because Ho like Jorge was a professional. The trap was now baited for the other American. Ho had studied them and knew they believed in their comrades perhaps as much or even more than the Vietnamese. The other one in the picture would come now for his friend. Ho was sure he had left no trail to where he was now hiding. He would rest for a few hours before finding and killing the other American. Ho was restless and could not sleep. The scouts had been out and reported that the Americans had left the area. Ho wanted some fresh air and went outside. He decided to backtrack to the tree where he left the American body tied to be sure he had left no trace of his path. He carried his AK47 and wore his knife on his belt.

The body was gone, good. The Americans had been there. They would return. He approached the tree cautiously and detecting nothing out of the ordinary he leaned his rifle against the tree and sat down to rest, think, and wait. As soon as he sat he realized he was sitting in a recess a human ass leaves where someone had very recently been sitting for a long time. He was sitting in the same exact same spot B.C. had vacated before climbing the tree.

Before Ho had a chance to move B.C. leaped out of the tree right on top of him. B.C. had his knife and immediately stuck Ho in the eye with it but before he could push it in Ho had grabbed the knife by the handle and was trying to pull it out. B.C reacted by trying to drive his thumb of his other hand thru Ho's other eye socket. Ho reacted by taking his other hand and began pushing two of his fingers thru one of B.C.'s eyes. B.C. reaction was to stop pushing on the knife for a split second and in that split second Ho took his hand that had been holding the knife, slid his hand to B.C.'s face and used his thumb to push out B.C.'s other eye. Both men were now blind.

There was no sound coming from either as they separated and rolled on the jungle floor trying to get an advantage in their eternal darkness and pain. They used knees and hands grabbing and punching in the dark. They became separated. Both were used to the dark tunnels, the pain in their eyes was something new. Neither realized at first they were blind. Both men lie on the jungle floor. The only sounds they heard was their heavy breathing from their close quarter fight. Realization of total darkness came at last to both. What, where and who they were slowly returned to them as their minds returned them from their animalistic fight of survival. Both men controlled their breathing as they moved off in their different directions.

Ho in the blackness crawled until he heard the footsteps of sandals on the forest floor. He knew these were the footsteps of his men so he quietly called out the password. The two Viet Cong heard him and carried him to hospital.

B.C. in his now forever darkness climbed back up the tree to await his fate. His fate was his returning unit looking for him. He signaled as soon as he heard the voices of Americans. He half fell, half jumped out of the tree not quite knowing for sure where the ground was and landed with a thud. He almost got shot but was thankfully recognized. The men thought it was his body that had fallen. They rolled him over to see one of his eyes lying on his cheek and a black empty hole where the other one had been. He was awake but said nothing. A medic bandaged him up, a medivac chopper was sent for and his war was over.

The Convergence of Diversity

Wars end. The two antagonist made their way to their prospective homes in divergent paths. One, the American, B.C. first went to the hospital in Japan before being shipped and discharged in Texas. He was given extensive training for the blind by the V.A. and the Disabled Veterans. B.C. not being a quitter by nature was determined no to be a cripple. B.C. obtained a braille computer and printer thru a private donation in his hometown of Midland, Texas. He taught himself to trade in the stock market. By now the people in power in Midland had heard of his war time exploits and being a very patriotic group at heart were more than happy to give him advice on the stock market. B.C. became a very wealthy man.

Ho by contrast was taken into the tunnel hospital where he was bandaged up. The United States had just started carpet bombing the Iron Triangle so the wounded were sent away as soon as it was possible. Ho was smuggled up the Saigon River via boat to the Ho Chi Minh Trail where he was taken overland north to his home in Hanoi. As soon as he was released from hospital Ho had nowhere to go and no one to go to. He became a beggar on the streets. One day when he was asking strangers for money or food one of his old comrades, Bao from the tunnels in Chu Chi saw him. His comrade knew the whole story about the fight that made him blind offered to set him up in business, the black market business. It seems there was a lucrative trade from South Vietnam to North Vietnam in American goods and money from corrupt officials in the South.

Ho's friend Bao had deep connections in the South because most of his family were from the Mekong Delta and were all members of the People' Liberation Front better known as the Viet Cong. Bao furnished Ho with American products to sell on the street. There was no prejudice against foreign goods on the streets. Ho made a living. He ate. He could afford a small room out of the elements. He even bought a pair of Foster Grant sunglasses for himself. They felt so much better than the cheap Russian pair he had no choice but to wear before. Ho's luck changed right after the fall of Saigon.

Bao's family went into the export business with a vengeance. Because they had been so loyal to the Communist they were now in a leadership position in the Mekong Delta. American goods, scrap metal and weapons headed north. Bao was overwhelmed with work and put Ho in the scrap metal business. Ho excelled and was soon a major player in providing metal, weapons, cars and trucks first in the North then in the South. Vietnam was one country now. Ho became a wealthy and respected man.

In the year 2010 while doing research for a book on the Tunnel Rats a writer named Mike Brumbley heard about the fight between B.C.and his adversary and the blinding of both. It was one of many stories of these extraordinarily two brave men Mike had heard. The story of both blinding each other had been stuck in Mike's mind ever since. He realized when he heard B.C.'s first statements made after the fight, "That son of a bitch got my eyes but I got his too. There's a blind gook running around somewhere. Fuck him wished I could have killed the bastard." that he had to tell their story. Two men fought not to their deaths but to the loss of their sight. Sometimes truth is stranger than fiction.

Mike was able to trace the command structure of the hidden NVA headquarters in the Iron Triangle and was able to find B.C.'s antagonist commander. Mike need a name and if possible where the man lived for the story he was writing. Ho's commander knew exactly who he was and where he was. He told the American writer all about Ho because of his reputation as an engineer in the tunnels. He was well versed in the story of the fight and told his version to the fascinated writer. Ho, he explained was now one of the most respected men in the whole of Vietnam. Ho was now a rich businessman and lived in Hanoi. Mike followed the trail to Hanoi, found Ho and interviewed him.

Mike now armed with his interview and B.C.'s name and hometown went to Midland, Texas, where he found the office of Travis Investments. After introducing himself he told of his finding of the man who had blinded him and read his interview to him. "I'll be damned. That was a long time ago. I have no remorse just trying to move on and live the best life I can."

"Well sir I've pitched an idea to Time magazine about forgiveness among two old veterans of the Vietnam War. They are willing to pay all expenses for you two to reunite and let me take pictures and write the story. It will be all expenses paid."

"Did you ask that old Commie bastard?'

"No, sir not yet. I only had the idea on the flight back to the states but like I said if you're willing Time likes the idea.'

"I'll think about it. Let me know what he says. One more thing do you want the meeting in the states or in 'Nam?'

"I thought pictures right where it happened with you both would be the way to go."

"Like I said. Let me know and I'll think about it."

Mike thru the Vietnamese Embassy made all the contacts and got all the permissions because Ho agreed to the meeting. B.C. flew to Hanoi where Mike met him and took him to a house he had rented for the two of them. Ho had agreed to meet them at the tunnel location. Mike had hired a Vietnamese tunnel guide from Chu Chi to get them as close as he could to where Ho killed the American with his AK47 then hung him from a tree and the fight had taken place. Both men were legends in their own theaters.

B.C. with Mike and their guide met Ho and his guide near a tunnel entrance that the guide said went to a dummy tunnel. There was also a hole big enough for a small man dug into the side of the tunnel wall. They were as sure as they could be about the location. A lot of the vegetation had changed and some of the tunnels were gone destroyed in the carpet bombing that followed the famous fight.

Neither man spoke. Neither was sorry or apologetic. After standing there in complete silence B.C. started walking until he felt a tree in his path with his cane. "This is the place. The place he hung my friend after carving him up. Tell that gook bastard I wish I had killed him."

The translator told Ho what the American had said. Ho smiled and stuck out his hand and said something in Vietnamese to his translator. The translator thought for a moment before speaking, "Now we understand each other you foreign pig. Your airplanes killed my family. I am blind. They say I am wealthy. I say I am poor. I took revenge for my family on you only because you were there. Mr. Travis the man has his hand out and wants to shake yours."

"Guide me to him Mike.' Mike took B.C. by the arm and guided his hand toward Ho's. B.C. took Ho's hand and the two just stood there hands embraced, staring into the nothingness before their eyes. "If you wanted more for your story Mike like smiling faces and warm embraces you're shit out of luck." Mike got his picture and his story. Time refused to print it because there was no story of forgiveness to be had between the two men shaking hands in the Vietnamese woods, only bad memories they both wished would have stayed where they belonged, in the past.

The End

The Death of Mr. Burrows

Back Door Man

"Boy, if you want me to talk turn that damn machine on and let's get on with it. I haven't felt myself lately and I might just drop dead any time. I'm getting old and my memory ain't what it used to be but I'll tell you what I know. Tell me again who sent you."

"Mr. Burrows, I was sent here by the Library of Congress to interview you about your life in and around White House politics for the last fifty years. It is well known five Presidents sought your advice and two even had an office for you to use. It is well known around Washington you were referred to as, *The Back Door Man*, because you shunned publicity."

"The country is in such a damn mess now it won't matter two shits what I say anyway. We my boy are on the edge of the abyss and the fall is a long way down. Too many smiling faced dumbasses in charge now taking bad advice. Is that damn machine on or not? I cuss a lot so get used to it. If you knew what I do any sane person would run out of adjectives and adverbs to define stupid!"

"Yes sir, it is recording. It's all yours."

"Then ask away young man. Let's get to it."

"I guess the best place to start is the, as they say the beginning."

"Ok boy now shut up and listen and I'll tell you about the abortive death of that devil democracy in America. I hope you know your history boy. I'll school you up as much as I can. We are a mirror of the past the good and the bad. America has had a lot of good luck and good leaders but now we are reflecting world politics more than our own grass roots brand. We are currently going thru the same fiasco of the English Parliament at the end of WWII."

"The Communist and the old school boys were fighting tooth and nail for control of the country. The English should get on their hands and knees and kiss Churchill's ass. He saved the country from them inbred Germans on the throne. You do know boy that the English and most of the rest of Western Europe are descended from the results of the wars with their native Celts and the wandering, warring Germanic tribes that conquered most of Europe. That makes most us white folks in America a bunch of Kraut eaters. We might have a touch of Roman in the mix from the Roman invasion but hell boy the Romans are themselves Trojans who migrated from Troy after their defeat by the Greeks. There was already settlements of Greeks in Italy and all of the above married into the Italian tribes. All of them mountain and sea people, tough as nails. I have to spit hand me something will you?"

" Fucking Communist are like flies on dead meat, They just want go away and if you leave them alone they infect everything. Share the wealth my ass. The Commies have as many fat cats as anybody else. Now the bastards are in our ghettos, universities, public schools and sad to say our government stirring up trouble. I'm sorry boy I get side tracked. You think the Chinese have space stations, space planes and stealth technology by accident? Bill Clinton listened to too many Doobie Brothers albums when he wasn't inhaling. Lying bastard. Fuck it. It's my death bed confession I'll say whatever I want. If you don't like it pack your shit and get. Now get me a sip of water."

"Yes sir, here's your water. I'm not here to judge. I was sent to record whatever you say sir. Please continue."

"The recent shit storm started with McCarthy. Political son of a bitch wanted headlines. He should have dealt with Hollywood at the negotiating table instead of on the damn television. He really got those Commie bastards worked up and they never forgave him. They just waited patiently for their turn and now their turn has come. Those hearings began the definition of the biggest threat to democracy that has ever existed, technology. Television started innocent enough, a sort of visual radio and like the movies pure entertainment then it was turned into a tool to control the fucking sheep. Now the bullshit is off the charts. You better believe boy that our people are sheep being led to the slaughter by selfish, lying bastards that don't give a shit. People with political agendas now control the "free press" in America. Scary as hell. We are one crazy bastard away from losing it all. Let me school you up."

"In capital letters written across the sky in capital letters, **DEMOCRACIES FAIL.** Ours almost did once by the Civil War. The War of Northern Aggression is what Southerners like to call the Civil War. This war was caused by and lies on the shoulders of a bunch of fanatical politicians kissing the ass of rich cotton planters. The politicians catering to the elite. Rich elitist bastards didn't like being told what to do. Sound familiar. Cotton was king. You can't imagine it now but South Carolina was the Kuwait of its day. The planters bought themselves a new country, The Confederate States of America."

"I traced my family back as far as 1741 in Virginia before I lost the trail. I am an American first. America was the country of my ancestors who many fought for and died for their efforts. Others were taken by disease, starvation, murder and a lucky few, old age. Old age to those folks was about forty. After the succession my family's country became the Confederate States of America. My family had finally taken roots in Tennessee after migrating from Virginia in around 1742 so we are Southerners thru and thru. The rich planter bastards and their paid politicians not only destroyed my new country but drug our home state of Tennessee down with it. The South has still not recovered."

The Rich Utopians

"Now boy right now in front of your eyes rich bastards having done their homework understand how to take over a democracy and are buying their technologies and politicians by the truckload. I guess you could call it a truckload sale. Ha! made a joke. The new prize is the whole of the United States of America. These people are worse than the planters. They want the whole enchilada and will use any means to get it. Their favorite tools have aways been the blacks and now with this new exodus of migrants of unknown origin or destination to America they have a whole new army of brown, black and yellow folks to help them along. These migrants are the new slaves of the Rich Utopians. The Communist are lost in their own rhetoric and are being used just like any other fringe group. Communist are as stupid as any other sheep. Rich Utopians seem to only be interested in the survival of their own species. The trick to the whole thing is simple, *Tell people what they want to hear.* The sheep of many colors will help the Rich Utopians achieve the domination and destruction of the Constitution of the United States. What a perfect emblem for the crazy bastards, a rainbow."

"The Rich Utopians want an experimental playground to move the fucking sheep around. Idiots there will never be a perfect world. It's against man's nature. They actually believe the world is black and white, 1 or 0. Sound the buzzer, **EEHHHHHH!,** Wrong answer. Humans live and work in the gray areas of survival and their passions. If the rich fuck up the country they smile, lie some more and move on. Maybe we'll do better the next time, drinks anyone. It has always been the poor to suffer and it always will be. Once the Rich Utopians get in charge if things go to hell in whorehouse U.S.A. they can always call in the U.S. Army which they now control to clean up the mess they created. Funny as hell how they are blaming Donald Trump for everything evil while the whole time they are the ones actually doing it. Brilliant. Technology and corruption working the sheep hand in hand for the good of us all. Should I puke or cry?

BAAA BAAA! The Army will have to obey because of their sworn oath. Bullets aren't prejudice, the person who pulls the trigger might be. Be something wouldn't it if we had a military coup to save our country? We are not immune, just think we are. What a racket for the Rich Utopians, protected on all sides! Win, win for the rich. Pop the corks and move on. Bastards, nosey, stupid, do gooder, thieving bastards!"

"I'm drifting again but the whole thing pisses me off. I'm going back to the Civil War. John Wilkes Booth fucked the South for good when he killed Lincoln. Lincoln wanted to ship the majority of the slaves out of the country because he knew the problems created by the freeing of so many dependent people on the populace. Look what's happening now in our modern times when the dumbest son of a bitch that ever lived, Joe Biden unleashed millions of poor people on his own country. Unbelievable. Why hasn't he been tried for treason. There I go getting off subject again. You do know old Abe was going to forgive the South and bring the country back together."

"It pains me to say it but Lincoln was a compromiser and a smart son of a gun. The rich vengeance filled Yankee businessmen licked their chops and went to work before he was even in the ground stealing my country. Them and the damn Englishmen made a fortune off of the slave trade, blamed it all on the South then they turn around and steal the whole South, lock stock and barrel. Like most despots eventually the Yankee businessmen over did it during Reconstruction. They pissed off the South so much that as soon as Reconstruction was over the Southerns went for the easiest target to blame for their troubles, the blacks. The rich Yankees and the English were to blame but the blacks were a closer and easier target. This started a whole new train of misery for the South both black and white and created a mess that we are still dealing with."

"That's my pill alarm going off. Hand me my pills. Thank You. Speaking of pills you do know that about half of our country is stoned all the time either on booze, illegal or legal drugs. Beware of any sober, disciplined enemy with a purpose and a will. He might just be a drug dealer or a pharmaceutical representative. Haha! That's a good one. The druggies are the living testament of the weaknesses and vanities of our people.You getting this?"

"Yes sir."

Thieves and Beggars

"The next big turd in the punchbowl of America was dear old Lyndon Johnson and his *War on Poverty* and the civil rights mess he started. There is no such thing as civil rights boy. Rights are what you earn by your actions not a gift. Rights do not come from some bought and paid for politician, no matter his good intentions. Johnson was acting like civil rights was manna from heaven, a gift he bestowed on the downtrodden. Hand me that garbage can boy I think I might puke. The *War on Poverty* on the surface I believe was with the best of intentions but unfortunately started the path of destruction of the poor by making them dependent on Uncle Big Tit. I know because I'm from Appalachia, the poorest area in the country. I know poverty. We were professionals at it in Appalachia. Johnson did this nonsense while fighting a war at the same time in Vietnam. Again our friend technology helped the Rich Utopians of America spread lies about the war by shifting focus on civil rights to buy time for the Communist. Johnson was the best press agent the Communist ever had. **Commies Never Sleep**, might be a good motto for them."

"It was about this time the Rich Utopians started another disloyalty program in our country by removing the pledge of allegiance and prayer from the schools. Can't have loyalty to the country or morality in school, God forbid. It's part of their destroy the foundations of the Constitution pogrom. Get rid of anything that has to do with republicanism or religion. The enemies of America can"t stand the words republic or God. The word **Democracy** covers all the bases for their ideology; to them the word democracy is equivalent to the words for religion and government all rolled into one neat package deal. Democracy now has left the realms of ideology and has crossed to the world of faith. The very word *republic* is now the new term for Satan among the Democratic faithful. The word makes them nervous as hell. Things are so screwed up and the sheep so brainwashed by technology they don't know their own country was founded as a republic not a democracy. Democracy what a fucking joke. Their thinking is if you breathe and look human you have all of these "rights". Pure destructive nonsense. The people that contribute and make their way deserve to be in charge. They are a proven commodity. Just get off your ass and contribute and the rewards will come. Why not just join in? It's easier. I'm really all over the place now ain't I. I've kept some of this bottled up in me so long it feels good just to let her rip. Consequences be damned. I'm going to switch gears again here boy and school you up."

"Ever here of the Byzantium Empire or Constantinople?"

"Yes sir. Byzantium was the Eastern Roman Empire and Constantinople was the capital."

"Well let me tell you how they fucked that up and now we are doing the same thing here and now. History does come around to bite us in the ass every now and then don't it boy? The Emperors were terrified somebody was going to screw the royal pussy and contaminate the bloodlines so they like the Egyptians before them brought in eunuchs to run the government on the theory that people with no balls wouldn't be a problem. They sure wouldn't be knocking up the royal snatch. Sound the buzzer again, **EHHHHHHH**! Wrong answer. The eunuchs still had working brains. Some even became great generals, teachers and administrators. They eventually took control of the running of the empire to the extent the Emperor was a figurehead, a yes man for those without balls. The bad news for the Emperor in his wisdom to protect royal pussy he forgot about the horny Viking palace guards who still had balls. Some were indeed getting the royal snatch. I wonder what the Eastern monarchs thought about the blond, blue eyed Viking looking babies in the royal nursery. Food for thought, eh bucko. Solve one problem, create two more. Way to go boys. Again the gray areas dominate human existence not the world of 1 or 0, all or none was truth. Truth is gray."

"Now what does all of that have to do with the good old USA you might ask. We have a parallel situation is the answer. Our problem is not eunuchs in government but queers who now run parts of our government. That's why we are having so much trouble now over the LGBT branch of the Communist News Network. Boy, don't we love that technology? I'll answer. You bet your ass as long as we are in control of what goes on it. The queers have been repressed in society forever so they kept their sex lives private if they wanted to succeed. Like most ambitious humans they are not stupid so over the years many homos are now in positions of authority. Like kind helps like kind. Get it. Their positions in society as a whole are now to the point they said to the general public. *enough is enough.* They came out in mass and made a political statement. The time was right with the touchy, feely sheep where everything goes, Rich Utopian crowd. Their use of technology with Hollywood as their ally for their, there's that word again, *rights,* was well conceived. Again 1 or 0, all or none. In the gray area most folks are too busy to care how many penises you take up the ass or beavers you eat but can't you keep it to yourself. It's how the queers are demanding and pushing is what pisses people off. Again the Communist in Hollywood are still pissed about McCarthy so are more than willing to help because there are so many homos in authority out there now. I'll give them folks a friendly piece of advice for free. How about that! I made a bunch of money off of advising dummies. Oh well. The homos better leave the kids alone. People will kill your ass if you indoctrinate their kids against their morality. Children are the line in the sand over this issue. That reminds me I heard something one time that makes a lot of sense to me. If my roof leaks I call a roofer. If my pipes leak I call a plumber. I don't recall ever needing an actor or an athlete to do anything except like a prostitute entertain me. Wish them dummies would get off the technology. It confuses the sheep."

"Who needs morals anyway. I got the answer boy. You do. I do. We all do. Where was I? Oh yeah. Now with so called civil rights the money printing machines are turned on full blast to educate the new oppressed people. Fine and good. nothing wrong with education. The problem the dumbasses created was that now they had all of these educated black folks who couldn't get a job. So where do they turn? The giant tit of course, the U.S. Government. Like the eunuchs and the queers the smart ones looked ahead, made their way, gained control and brought in their cronies to the point the blacks are now the defacto power behind the throne in Washington and everybody in that town knows it. The problem is they got there by whining and begging. I would have admired the bastards more if they had said enough is enough and picked up a gun and went somewhere and started their own county, Now that would have gained respect. Any more I'm out of the judging business, too old. It's just the way it is. The problem that scares me the most is that Communism because of all the hate that has been generated over real or imagined events revenge has taken over many blacks as a philosophy to overcome the wrongs they believe occurred in their past. Like I said whiners and beggars. Europeans were slaves for thousands of years and moved on. ***Maybe think about it's time to move on.*** The Rich Utopians couldn't be happier than a dog rolling in a pile of cow shit. More radical bullshit. Everybody except the rich has problems. The rich will tell you they have problems too. I bet any poor son of a bitch in the country would gladly trade their problems for a rich mans any day of the week. Life has no guarantees. Earn your way then you can smile in your coffin. I guess I just have always hated beggars and thieves. Right now our country is being stolen in the biggest robbery in world history because of beggars of all descriptions and corrupt politicians. Make your way. If you do well good for you. If you don't, smile and go on but don't beg. I got a good story for you about beggars and bums but first I got to go piss."

"My own mother used to tell my kin folks I was a bum. When I was a young man I went off to war and met people from all over the U.S. I thought they were interesting as hell and what a big and diverse country we had and I wanted to see it when I got out. I have to get something off my chest right now before I forget my train of thought. All of these idiots walking around now with guns and talking about a civil war do not have a clue what they are talking about. I have seen the piles of American dead killed in battle and I don't like it. War is the last thing you ever want. War is the ultimate political tool. War is not a fucking movie. Anyway the bum story, I wanted to see the country when I got out of the service and now I had friends all over the country. I saved my money and stuck out my thumb and took off. I drifted around the country for years working every kind of shit job known to man to survive, visited friends and really saw our country from the ground up. Met all kinds of people: rich, poor, famous, crazy and everything in between. Found out race or status has pretty much nothing to do with being a decent human being or a cretin. There are as many nice rich folks as there are poor, same with the mean son of a bitches and the crazies. It you ask me its a pretty well balanced distribution. Haha! I made another joke. What no sense of humor? The thing I decided I had in common with the folks I met was the fact we were all Americans united by a bond of unspoken commonality of our past and a belief in a future. Sorry mom I wasn't a bum. I was only curious."

"Not sure I'm even making sense. I know I'm rambling but

you're the one that asked me and I always liked to talk. I can't emphasis enough that democracies fail. Ask the Greeks who invented it, the Germans, the Russians, the Chinese, the Southerns in our own country and on and on. They will tell you it's a matter of time. Republics have a much better record of survival. I got another little historical goodie for you about good old Julius Caesar."

"He was broke and needed the money to bribe Senators to get himself elected. I'm sorry I don't remember for what position. No matter how much he borrowed he couldn't get enough to buy his way in, then he had a brilliant idea. He didn't need to bribe the Senators he had only to bribe the vote counters when the tribes voted. The tribes were the Roman equivalent of our Electoral College. He won. Smart son of a bitch. That story should sound familiar because of the mess of our last national election. Don't ever let the bought puppets of the Rich Utopians fuck with our Electoral College or our Supreme Court. They are all you have brother, all you have to save your ass in a pinch. I see old Hillary Clinton on tv every now and then complaining about them. Wish that old cunt would move on to the old folks home. All she has to offer is more totalitarian, Rich Utopian horse manure. These fuckers never give up. You people need to make up your minds if you love your home or not before you lose it all. See thru the smoke and mirrors. All big problems are a series of small problems. Solve the small problems, the big problems get eaten away piece by piece. Have a morality, respect others, love your country or get the fuck out. No one owes you a damn thing. BAAA BAAA! Now get out of here and leave me alone. I'm tired and want to die in peace. If I'm still alive come back tomorrow."

"Good morning young man. You came back. Bad news I'm still on this side of the dirt."

"Yes sir, I'm here until you tell me we are done."

"Fire up that machine and let's get it on. This is fun. If I get I'll piss off all kinds of folks when this comes out. Fuck 'em. America is more important than all the politicians that ever existed. Funny thing I woke up thinking about a rock and roll song my daughter used to play on her CD player so loud you could hear it all over the house. I don't remember the first words but the singer is screaming something about "here we are now entertain us". I thought it was a perfect motto for running for public office. Just like fucking kids, beggars and whiners gimme, gimme, gimme until it's all gone. If this is ever published do you think it will be burned or banned under one of our newer emerging *technological democracies* with its totalitarian government that is coming to America. If the sheep won't leave the corral we're all headed to the slaughter pens."

"Everything is so big now it's to the point of not being manage-able. Washington has become the enemy of their own people. Any person growing up like I did and where I did really understands the few free Americans left will be the new Indians for the Rich Utopians to round up and put on a reservation. Yahoo! Ride 'em cowboy. Our country needs to dismantle that giant hypocrisy in Washington and return the power to the states where it belongs. Washington, protect our borders and our land and let the states be in charge of themselves. If a state turns to despotism support the citi-zens to get rid of it. Everything in politics is simple human behavior hidden under piles and piles of bullshit. If the country is working let it alone and please shut off the money machine for a while. I remember the old timers use to warn us about putting fluoride in the water on a national level and about the insurance companies mandating seat belts and we made fun of them. Don't worry old timers. It's for the good of us all. One old man told me how stupid I was that once Washington started telling everybody what to do they would never stop. Seems like small potatoes now but at the time the issues were a big deal. The old men were right. Totalitarians do want to control every aspect of our lives. The word freedom has become an abstraction to manipulate. If people don't start putting the country first, protecting their history and heritage, practice some form of morality the game is over. A good place to start is to get young, healthy people off the government tit and show them how to prosper and the choice to use it or not. One more important piece of history I want to share before I go. This really, really pisses me off. Speaking of piss, hand me that urinal. Good boy. Ahhh! To dribble or not to dribble, that is the question? Feeling good now. Let's rip some more assholes shall we young man?"

"The same people that used to spit on the soldiers returning from Vietnam now have raised children and grandchildren and have taken over the politics of the entire West Coast, New York and D.C. It's a sad state alright. Don't ever forget the old Roman saying, "Who ever rules the mob, rules." Very appropriate don't you agree? When humanity reaches an apex of civilization it seems to have a need to destroy itself. We are not immune from history. Like I said we are but a reflection. Participate, learn and for God's sake protect the Constitution. It is the most valuable document ever conceived by man for the welfare of the common man. You were handed political freedom on a silver platter. What you do with it is up to you. Once the Constitution is gone. God help us all. Mankind may never see its like again. How can any fool compare it to a book on German economics as a comparative philosophy? Cut out this race based nonsense and hire the best to do the job and for the sake of the country get into those ghettos, universities, and public schools and root out the Communist and influence of the Rich Utopians if you want to save your country. Keep your eye on the prize boy. Stop treating our sacred land like a giant whorehouse would be a good place to start. Everybody wants a piece of the richest country in the world. Once it's gone it's gone. I don't know if I made sense or not or if I said what you wanted to hear. You wouldn't believe what I said to some of our clueless leaders but I will take that to the grave. I gave you the outline. You fill in the blanks. What are they going to do kill me? Ha! Now get out of here and don't come back. I think soon it's time for me to die. BAAA BAAA!"

"Yes sir, It's time for you to die alright sir"; with that the CIA man put the pillow over the old man's face and pressed down until he didn't feel any movement. He returned the pillow, checked the old man's pulse, picked up the recording device and walked out the door. Before leaving he had taken one last look at the old man's body. leaned over and whispered in the never to hear any more words ear from Presidents or anyone else, "FYI sir, I am a registered Democrat, your jokes suck and I like lamb chops."

The End

The RV (Resurrection Vehicle)

Snowbirds

Dell Hicks looked out the window of his Goodie's Travel Trailer Park office window to see the beginnings of yet another beautiful autumn morning. The leaves were getting that hint of color to let everyone know a change was coming. The morning birds were in full symphony in the trees and all was well in Dell's world. He noticed that overnight the biggest, blackest and one of the most beautiful self contained rv's he had ever seen had pulled in to lot 7 in the back. Driving it was a repeat customer from a few years ago, one Alexander Kroic.

This thing was something special. Dell was sure this huge trailer could not be classified an rv, probably better to call it a motor home or even a bus; to Dell it looked like one of those fancy buses the country singers traveled in when on concert tour. It was a complete custom made job.

It was massive. A complete self contained home away from home on wheels. The owner had to be rich, that's for sure. This same trailer had been here a few years ago and the owner had requested online the same space in the rear of the park he had had rented previously. Alex as he insisted on being called on his first visit followed the same procedure to register this time as he had used before: everything done online, paid in full. Dell remembered Alex as a quiet, polite man keeping to himself. Free Country.

Dell remembered the man from his last stay as being a bit of a night owl, sleeping during the day. Alex had been seen on several occasions at all hours of the night by Dell and some of the winter guest going for walks down the county road that ran in front of the park or going into the woods behind his trailer. He was always friendly, polite and sociable to Dell and the guest. He had refused several invitations to eat dinner with Dell or any of the long term snowbirds the last time he was parked here but he had joined in a few evenings of cards with some of the men. Alex was a teetotaler and never accepted a beer or a cocktail at any of the card games. Alex never spoke of his work or family. There had been a lot of speculation thru the snowbird community about both subjects, his obvious wealth and his heritage. Try as they might no consensus could be reached because no one could get more than a few vague utterances out of Alex about his past. Alex was a very private person. Alex was finally labeled an eccentric recluse and left alone. "I sure couldn't live like that, could you boy?" muttered Dell to his German Rottweiler, Red.

"What's a matter boy? A deer in the woods." Red had been acting peculiar and as soon as Dell opened the back door Red had just sat there staring thru the glass of the storm door towards the woods. Dell had opened the door more than once to let him out but

Red wouldn't go out. He just stood there staring. When Dell finally shut the back door Red let out a small whimper and returned to his favorite spot on the couch and commenced chewing on his favorite old shoe. Twice when Red had to go out to do his business he went to the front door, finished then returned straight to the house. Red never went to the front door when wanting to go outside to do his business and he always liked to scratch his back in the grass and lie in the warm sun for a spell before returning to the indoors but not this time. "I guess we're both getting peculiar in our old age. Ain't we boy? I better go out and clean up your dog shit off of the front yard in case folks come over. What's a matter boy? Not feeling well. I'll take you to the vet if you don't get better." Dell was thinking that his crazy dog probably ate something else again not fit for consumption and his stomach was acting up. "Please old buddy don't puke in the house like the last time when you ate part of that blanket. I sure would appreciate it."

Dell had been right about Alex's custom rv's classification. It was in fact a custom built bus, air tight with all the latest security including reinforced doors, bulletproof blackened windows, surveillance cameras and touch sensors. Alex had spent a fortune on generators that could run on either propane or rechargeable batteries with backups three layers deep. The setup included reversible solar panels on the roof and flywheel generators used for charging when driving. The custom interior lighting cost as much as some people's homes. What Alex had built for himself was not a self contained bus but a self contained coffin where he could sleep in relative peace and darkness during the day. Alex had been dead for over three thousand years. Alex was tired of being dead. He knew life was long gone from this meat sack he was stuck in. Alex coveted the thing he was most afraid of, final peace. His animal lust demanded blood and life while what remained of his humanity sought tranquility, the tranquility of eternal rest. What Alex desired most of all was to be gone forever, like dust in the wind.

Dell couldn't sleep for worrying about Red. It was 2:45 in the a.m. and he was wide awake. He made himself get up. The first thing Dell did every time he left the comfort of his warm bed was to put on his furry house shoes to protect his feet from the cold floors. He sat on the edge of the bed for a moment gathering his senses and listening for Red. Red who he could tell by his breathing was fast asleep. Lucky bastard thought Dell as he put coffee in the electric coffee pot. He was wide awake now. I might as well do something he thought to himself. He poured his first cup of coffee, sat at the kitchen table and stared out the storm window that faced the back of the house. He watched as Alex exited the rv door and walk straight for the woods. "What the hell," Dell said to his sleeping dog. Dell picked up his binoculars and looked at the place Alex had entered the woods. Nothing. Dell between sips of coffee would ever so often take another look at the woods thru his binoculars. Once he thought he saw a dog but he wasn't sure. "I'm up now Red, might as well cook some breakfast." As Alex was washing his dishes from breakfast he noticed Alex returning from the woods. Dell glanced at the time on his phone. It was 4:47 in the a.m. Alex appeared to be in no hurry; in fact Alex sat down on the wooden picnic table at lot number 7 and looked to the East. Alex was doing something, looking for those first tell tale signs of the dawn. His signal to return to his coffin on wheels.

Dell didn't think Alex was a thief. He hadn't carried anything in to the woods with him to bury or to dig up something from his last visit to the park. What in the world would a full grown man want in the empty woods for two hours on a dark cold night. "I bet he's a hunter or a tree hugger checking out the game. That's got to be it boy. The deer are moving at night more than ever because of all the noise in the woods from the hunters. As it got closer to dawn the deer would be moving back from grazing and drinking to a bed ground. Jesus, Red I just realized how much I talk to my dog."

Yes Dell, the deer were moving and Alex was hunting. Alex stripped off his clothes, folded them neatly, laid them on a rock by the pond he was standing by and evoked his Romanian wolf spirit. His hybrid body now in the shape of part wolf, part man went hunting. The wolf half of Alex picked up the scent of a buck that had left his piss sign on a tree. The eyes of the human half saw the buck's tracks in the soft, damp earth. No other bucks had challenged him yet so he was alone. There was a fainter scent of doe piss on the trail. The buck was following a herd of doe. Alex the living dead was thirsty for blood, deer blood. Alex the wolf was hungry for meat. Alex was a hunter, a good one.

Human blood was not relevant in this hunt. Humans were just prey to him, their blood satisfying his living dead human half while the meat satisfied the wolf. Alex had been a human once so he knew how to hunt them. The wolf hunted the game in the forest driven by pure instinct, the instinct of survival. Alex liked variety in his blood lust. Alex drained the buck of blood and satiated with his need for meat returned to where he left his clothing by the pond, washed the blood from his body, dressed and walked back to his coffin.

Later that morning Dell's curiosity got the best of him. An hour after daybreak he went for a look see in the woods. Maybe old Alex was right there might be some big bucks in those woods. Dell used to hunt but had lost interest in about everything he did after his sweet Rebecca had passed away from that devil cancer. What Alex found made him run back to the house and call the game warden. "Bob this is Dell. I think I found something that might be that CWD (Critical Wasting Disease) that's spreading around the country. It's not like anything I've ever seen. A completely healthy looking buck in his rut that looks like he's been bled but there's no blood on the ground. You better hurry. I think the wild dogs have found him as something had ripped open it's throat and a big chunk of hindquarters is all chewed up."

"Good morning to you to Dell. I'll send out somebody to look as soon as I can. Hunting season is going strong so we are running around like chickens with our heads chopped off. As usual too many hunters, too few game wardens. Seriously Dell thanks for calling, without people like you watching and helping us out we would be in even a worse mess. If I can't get somebody out there today I'll come by myself after work and have a look see and collect some samples. Thanks again and give Red a kiss for me will you?"

"Fuck off, Bob." Just like he promised after work Bob drove up and parked in empty lot 8 next to the biggest, fanciest motor home he had ever seen. Dell watched him enter the woods. Bob followed

Dell's instructions on how to find the buck's body. He took pictures of the buck, pictures of foot prints around the buck, samples of the deers: skin, meat, brain and liver and bone. Bob would investigate the tracks while sending the samples to the state lab for evaluation. Bob took one look at the tracks and scratched his head. If it's a dog it's got to be the biggest one in the county. The claws and front pads were huge and the animals weight was not on them.The deepest part of any print was where an animal put its weight. The back of the print that was from a dog was normally the faintest; on this dog it was the deep point with an almost human looking shape. He had better warn folks to be on the lookout for a huge wild dog running around. Bob from years of experience didn't panic but instead got on the internet and began doing his homework. The closest thing he could find to his track was that of an extinct wolf from the forest of the mountains of Eastern Romania but still something was just not right. If this was a Romanian wolf which was impossible, it was a big as a man. I'll change my warning to either a wild dog or a wolf.

Red didn't seem any worse than normal. His appetite was good. He was peeing and shitting the same as always. He drank normal amounts of water. Dell based this evaluation on the amount of Red's drool that flowed out of his mouth moving from the water bowl to the couch. For some crazy reason he still wouldn't go out the back door. He would only stare, sometimes with a whimper and sometimes in a semi-agitated state but he absolutely refused to go out that back door. Dell would open the front door, Red would run out, do his business then stand and scratch on the front door until Dell opened to let him in.

Bob called Dell two days later and told him what he had found out about the dead buck. This was not CWD case, no evidence at all. The missing blood had to be explained by the wild animals lapping it up. What else could it be? Nothing else made sense. This site was just a freak occurrence. "Dell I'm putting out a warning to the county to be on the lookout for a large wolf. I wouldn't go into those woods for a while or if you have to carry a gun. This wolf is a big one."

"A wolf! Good lord the wolves have been gone from this country for years. Way back in the day. How could it be a wolf."

"If I have to guess some old boy tried breeding wolves or wolf dog crosses and one got away or he turned one out. You and I go way back so this one is off the record. The closest thing I can find to the prints is a Romanian wolf that has been extinct for a million years or so. Whatever this critter is he's a big one. I'd keep Red close for a while. It's your park but I'd tell them guest of yours to keep there pets under watch for a while and don't go on nature hikes in the woods. I know you so I'm sure you can think of the appropriate line of bullshit to tell them."

"Ok Bob. thanks for letting me know." Red not feeling well now this. "I guess my sleeping days are over for a while boy. You know me boy when I've got things on my mind I can't sleep worth a darn." True to his prediction about sleep Dell was wide awake even though it was 1:00 in the a.m. "Fuck it, I'm up." Dell put the coffee on and went to his favorite spot at the kitchen table, played with his coffee cup and stared out the window. Dell smiled when he heard Red fart in his sleep. There he goes again thought Dell as he watched Alex walk to the front of the park and down the county road. Dell grabbed his binoculars and watched Alex disappear in to the night. Dell thought he had seen a bird or maybe a bat fly off before he finally sat his binoculars down. "Shit, I forgot to warn him about the wolf. I can either get dressed and go out in the cold and try and find him or sit here in my warm kitchen drinking coffee. Tough decision huh Red." Dell continued to sit at the table until he got tired of sitting there then moved over to his recliner. Dell immediately fell asleep. He woke with a start, confused for a moment about where he was. He looked across at the clock on the wall and it was 4:30 in the a.m. From Dell's vantage point in his recliner he could see out of his front window and watched as a lone man walked down the county road and into the park. Must be Alex he thought. I'm going to print up some handouts tomorrow warning the guest to keep their pets close for a while. He would drop them off personally to help give that little homey feeling that so many of them liked.

Dell walked the park visiting his guest, talking to those that were home and leaving his print outs for those that weren't. Inside the window on the door to Alex trailer was a sign, **Day Sleeper Do Not Disturb.** Dell left his flyer and went home to Red. Alex had been busy the night before.

Dell had in deed seen something flying in the night sky. It was a bat, a very big bat. Alex had crossed a fence, disrobed in an empty grain silo. Alex left the silo by flying out a hole in the roof. Alex was using his search radar to scan for warmth. Warm meant life was near. If it was the warmth radiating from a living being that meant warm blood. Alex found what he was looking for. Alex had detected the warmth coming from several cattle and a horse but Alex flew on. He was thirsty for human blood. The buck had satisfied his blood lust but human blood was the sweetest of all. He was a connoisseur of the precious warm liquid he needed to survive.

Bobby left the car running to keep the heater and radio on while he made out with Judy in the back seat. Alex flew onto the top of the car and hit with a thud. He had used this technique before. Sometimes it worked and sometimes it didn't. When teenagers were in parked cars late at night the responses were pretty much the same everywhere. They would either get scared and tear out of there fast or lost in their passions just ignore the sound. Car loads of teen boys out partying late could go in all kinds of directions; if they were drinking or smoking pot all bets were off. Alex had been to this part of the country before.

The last time Alex had stayed at Dell's rv park when he had been out hunting for blood a teen had stuck a pistol out of a pickup passenger side window, pointed it straight up and then proceeded to empty the magazine into the empty darkness. Only the night sky wasn't empty. He perhaps made the unluckiest shot anyone would ever make. Alex was circling above having detected warmth emitting from humans that would occasionally exit the pickup. Alex was shot in a wing. Alex not expecting anything to happen to him fell straight out of the sky and this time hit not a vehicle but the ground with a thud. He flopped around until he regained control of himself. He lie there for a moment regaining his composure as he used the healing abilities of his mind to repair the wing. This had never happened to him before. He had always been so careful and methodical. Alex now had a choice, revenge or patience. He chose both. Alex was above all else hungry for life sustaining blood.

Alex flew back to a tree near the pickup from where the shot s had came. He hung upside down from one of it's branches, keeping his search radar on as he patiently waited for one of the teens to emerge from the truck or for the truck to leave. It wasn't long before a drunk teenager got out of the passenger side of the truck and stumbled into the woods apparently to take a piss. Alex dropped to the ground, shape shifted to his wolf person and attacked the young man ripping out his throat in an instant. Alex then had an orgy of violence against the young man as he ate his flesh, drank his blood and mutilated his corpse. The drunk teens in the truck started yelling for their friend to return. It was then that the wolf Alex emerged from the woods. He jumped upon the hood of the truck. That was all it took for the boys to put the pickup in reverse, hit the accelerator and got the hell out of there. Alex wasn't worried about showing himself to the frightened boys. Who would believe a bunch of drunk, stoned teenagers that a large wolf had jumped on their truck? Wolves had been gone from this part of the country for a long, long time.

Alex jumped from the hood and as soon as the truck was out of sight returned to human form, picked up what was left of the boy's body and ran with it in super human speed to the barn where he had left his clothing. Alex looked around the old barn until he found what he was looking for, a five gallon can of gas. Alex took out the gold lighter he always kept in the pocket of his trousers to light the barn on fire. The lighter had been a gift from a Middle Eastern potentate many centuries ago. It was a favorite souvenir of his. Alex's hobby for the last two thousand years, more or less, was the collection of valuable relics from his victims. If any item in particular caught his eye Alex kept it in his private collection now worth several million dollars. Alex had actually liked the rich young Middle Eastern man before he killed and ate him.

Alex poured the gasoline over the remains of the boy's body and lit the fire that would consume both the body and the barn.walked away in the total darkness of the night back to the Goodie's Travel Trailer Park where his traveling coffin would be waiting for his return. He as always read the sign, **You Are Not A God,** before retiring for the day. The next day the local papers, tv news and social media had two big stories, **Local Boy Missing After Wild Night Out** and **Sam Arnold's Barn Burns**, **Arson Suspected.**

The here and now would be a repeat performance of violence. Bobby thought he heard a tree limb hit the top of the car. He paused and looked up for just a second before going back to the task at hand. Bobby was too busy to be distracted by such a trivial thing as a dead limb falling from a tree. He put his face back between Judy's legs. Too bad he hadn't realized that where they were parked there were no trees within twenty yards of their car. Judy heard it to, "What was that?"

"Nothing.", mumbled Bobby from his position between Judy's legs, his face buried deep in her abundant pubic hair. Bobby added a quick, "I love you baby.", and it was back to work. Judy was not so sure it was nothing and ordered him to stop and take her home. It was time to go as far as she was concerned.

"Take me home now Bobby.", came her command to her horny, boyfriend.

"I got to piss." Bobby opened the car door and as soon as he did a wolf jumped on his back from the roof of the car and killed him in one bite by crushing his skull. Alex then jumped into the car and over the back of the front seat to kill then eat Judy after draining her blood. When Alex finished with the young lovers he retained his human shape, put Bobby's body in the back with Judy and drove the car to a local abandoned rock quarry where he had stashed his clothes. He drove the car to a ledge above the waiting waters that now filled the quarry and pushed the car over the edge into the darkness of the deep watching until it sank out of sight. Alex washed his body, returned to the grail silo, dressed and ran back to Dell's rv park. The next evening Alex without saying a word to Dell drove off in his bus.

You Are Not a God

You Are Not A God was a sign Alex kept hanging on the wall next to where he slept to remind him who he was. Alex always read it before returning to sleep. He personally had known one of the Roman Emperors. When the man was parading in his chariot after a victorious campaign through the streets of Rome a slave would ride behind him whispering, "You are a mere mortal, not a God.", to help him keep things in perspective. How bloody appropriate thought Alex. A little reminder to keep you focused. I'm sure the temptation to think one was a God could be overwhelming to a man who literally had everything in the pagan world. It would have been easy for someone in his unique position to think of themselves as a God.

The next day the news about the missing teens and the report of blood found on the ground in the county where the kids liked to park and make out was all the local community could talk about. The local papers, tv and social media were abuzz trying desperately to help in the search for the two missing teenagers and their car. Some thought they had eloped but those closest to the pair said no way. As with most excitement things would finally cool down after no trace could be found of the pair. Local law enforcement said that they had several good leads they were pursuing. Don't give up and give us time to do our jobs was all they would officially comment.

Dell was bored. Red was doing better. One winter day he was sitting peacefully in his recliner watching a rerun of "Law and Order", for what must have been at least the third time if not more and during an idle moment between commercials out of the blue said to Red, "That sure was funny wasn't it boy the last time that big black bus was here that other kid disappeared." Dell then had what some may call an epiphany others a brain fart. "Wait a minute. I'm right ain't I boy something bad happened the time before when that bus was here? A missing kid or a house or barn burned, boy." Dell went over to his computer, logged on and changed his life forever.

Dell was now in full detective mode. He got out a pad and pen and started taking notes. He wrote down the dates of Alex's visits and the bad things that had happened in the area on those dates. Dell expanded his search. He made a list of all the Goodie Travel Trailer sites around the country. He searched the online newspapers for any mysterious disappearances, animal mutilations, murders or arson in those same cities and the dates they occurred for at least the last three years. Dell got on the Goodie Association website where the owners communicated with each other and announced to his embarrassment he was having trouble with the IRS and needed the records of all the trailers that had visited his park for the last three years. Dell confessed to being a lousy bookkeeper and asked for help with some registration information of a few of the repeat customer or snowbirds that travelled their parks. He gave out the name of three guest including one Alex Kroic. If any of the three are current guest of yours if you wouldn't say anything to them I would appreciate it, I'm too embarrassed. "Throw 'em off the scent 'eh boy. No use spooking old Alex if he's around."

Dell took some ribbing from some of the owners he knew well. It was all in fun so he took it with a grain of salt. Dell got what he was looking for, the dates Alex Kroic visited their parks. Dell began to troll the waters of the online and social media world looking again for any mysterious events in those towns or cities on the dates Alex had been in their community. When Dell had enough information he went back to his list. His arthritic hands began to cramp from all of the typing and writing. Dell sat back in his chair looking at his finished work. "Damn Red. This dog don't hunt. No way this is coincidence. No way. Well boy I'm calling Uncle James and he'll be watching you and the park for a few days. I've got to take a trip." Dell called his uncle, packed, put his binoculars in the glove box of his old pickup, threw his bag in the back, and headed for Las Vegas.

Mr. Entertainment

Alex was at the Goodie's Death Valley RV Park outside of Las Vegas, Nevada. Dell found a room at he Holiday Inn near the Las Vegas Sphere. Dell was fascinated by this bit of technology. When he wasn't doing anything else, which was most of the time, he would watch it for hours. Amazing.

Dell had scouted out the park. Alex was there. The black beast bus wasn't hard to miss even among the plethora of rich people's buses at the park. Dell was staying hidden from the park owner whom he had known for years. It would save a whole bunch of unnecessary lies and the chance of being found out by Alex. As the sun was getting low Dell drove into the hills surrounding the Goodie Park and found a good place where he could watch Alex's bus at night. He laid his binocs on a rock and waited for Alex to emerge from his bus. The park was well lit so he would be able to see when Alex exited the bus.

True to form at 1:15 a.m. Alex stepped out of his bus and walked to a gate that allowed the guest access to a hiking trail that wound it's way thru the desert. The moon was full and in the reflections coming from the white sands Alex was easy to follow until he went over a hill into a depression. A few minutes lated a large bat flew out of that same depression. Dell tried to follow the bat with his binocs but the bat's erratic pattern made it impossible. Dell once again focused on the last place he had seen Alex but after an hour he had not emerged. "Where could that bastard have gone?", Dell asked to the wind. I'm so use to talking to Red even when he ain't here I'm talking to myself.. A sure sign of getting old I reckon.

"I'm right here behind you Mr. Hicks." Dell thought he would have a heart attack right on the spot. The urge for fight or flight overtook him. The blood rushed out of his face and he was as pale as a ghost. His knees grew weak and his legs began to shake from the combination of fear and adrenalin. A completely nude Alex Kroic was standing there in the flesh. "Mr. Hicks breathe easy and regular now. It is not your imagination or a dream. I am real and I am standing here. If I wanted to kill you it would have already happened and you would have not known anything. Let that sink in Mr. Hicks. I will wait for you to speak. Do not run. If you do I will kill you. I have something to say to you. I have tried many times to speak to a human to make them an offer. All of my attempts have failed. I will let you live and I will disappear if you will just listen. If you try and tell this story no one will believe you anyway. I will simply disappear. You will be thought a lunatic. Please now breathe and I will wait."

The shaking Dell, who wanted more than anything to run away, wasn't sure he could trust his rubbery legs to work. All Dell could do was get out a feeble, "OK."

"Good Mr. Hicks. Your color is returning. When you are ready I will speak and you will listen."

"OK"

"I am over three thousand years old. I am a spirit walking in a human sack of meat and bones. I'm sure you suspect by now that something is amiss or you would not be here. We will assume I am correct in all points. Agree Mr. Hicks?"

"OK", and then it just came out, "Call me Dell."

"Good. I will continue. I cannot kill myself. I am a killer not by choice but driven by a passion to survive. I need blood like you need air. I want a human to kill me. I am tired Dell, so tired. I am in an eternal purgatory that will last for eternity unless I can end it. I will reward the person that becomes my advocate with my massive fortune. I wish we were in one of your American movies about vampires and you could just come into the bus and drive a stake in my heart and all would be well as you ride into the sunset. Sorry it will not be that easy."

"OK, I'm trying to listen."

"I have to do something first before we can plan my demise. There is a man in Las Vegas. I know you have heard of him he goes by the nickname of, *Mr. Entertainment.* I trusted him and I shouldn't have. I trusted him and gave him too many of the secrets of the living dead. He has betrayed that trust. I have to kill him before I die. If he is left alive after I am gone your world is in for a lot of trouble. I had to give up my humanity as the animal in me grew stronger out of necessity. Mr. Entertainment is the opposite. He enjoys and exploits human weaknesses especially those of greed and vanity. He is an expert in both as they are his own frailties. His desires will be his downfall. He is a dangerous spirit for humans to contend with. I have to deal with him. He still trust me. He believes us to be allies."

"I will contact you again soon; in the meantime enjoy your stay in Las Vegas, stay away from me and do not for any reason go near, *Mr. Entertainment.* If my plan works I will achieve peace and you will become a very rich man Dell, a very rich man indeed. I am going to disappear now. I want to leave you with something as a reminder this was not a dream and is serious business." Alex walked over to where Dell was sitting. The closer he got the harder Dell's body would shake. Alex bent over Dell, extended his hand and struck with lightening speed. Alex had replaced the finger nail on his forefinger with a claw. He cut Dell's face below his left eye to the corner of his mouth, a superficial wound but every time Dell looked into a mirror he would be reminded of this meeting.

The next night Alex walked into the penthouse suite of his protege, "Good Evening, Marcus or should I say, *Mr. Entertainment.*"

"Alex my old friend. What brings you here."

"I haven't seen you in a long time, so here I am."

"I'm having a private party tonight. You are invited. It will be a feast. Literally dozens of young, beautiful women, transients looking for fortune or fame. It's heaven for men with our taste."

"I've kept tabs on you my young friend. Do be careful Marcus. I doubt if there are any virgins in the lot and the drugs Marcus, don't you worry about contaminated blood?"

"I try and avoid the druggies but they are so prevalent now it's hard to catch them all. If I detect drugs I spit out the blood and move on."

"Cancel your party Marcus. I have a surprise for you. I have found a beautiful young virtuous girl, a true virgin. I want you with me tonight when I drain her. I have watched your progress from afar for over two hundred years my friend and it is time for you to move on to yet greater things. How do you think I've lasted so long my friend? I will make you practically invincible!"

"Tell me what you need of me Alex."

"It is time for your final transition. You are still a baby compared to me. I want to see the old country. I'm going back to Eastern Europe and the Mid East. The Americas will be yours from now thru eternity but before I leave there is one more ceremony to endure. I went thru it and so must you. The blood of a virgin is required. We my friend will rule the earth, an endless feast of meat and blood. What could be better?"

"Of course Alex of course. You are my mentor. I am your student. Come my friend let us go." The penthouse was locked, security was told to admit no one under any circumstance. Two men stood on the terrace of the upscale penthouse, stripped off their clothes and flew into the dry Las Vegas night.

Marcus followed Alex to the open window of a small house in North Las Vegas. The night air was still hot from the burning day. The migrant family had no ac. A small fan sat on a nightstand next to a sleeping girl. The two bats walked thru the open window. They transformed and now two completely naked men stood over the bed of the girl. She seemed to be about thirteen or fourteen which meant she menstruated. Alex had assured Marcus that she was as the old monks used to say, intacto. So quick it was undetectable by the human eye Alex punctured the girl's carotid artery with an elongated fingernail on his left hand. As the pulsating blood spilled onto the girl's t-shirt, "Drink this blood Marcus and I will say that if God is not dead he is asleep. Let him sleep on while we rule the earth. God is not needed. Drink so I can drink of her next and then we shall share each others blood to finish your transition. In effect you will be as powerful as me from this night on." Alex used Marcus vanity and greed against him. Marcus bent over the sleeping girl and began to drink from her neck. Marcus was consumed by his lust for the girl's blood. Alex had been in this room before and had secreted a garrote on a shelf of clothing above the girl's bed and a vile of herbs under the girl's mattress. As Marcus consumed the life giving blood Alex told him, "Save some for me my friend we both have to have her blood in our veins." Marcus reluctantly pulled his teeth from the girls neck and as soon as his lips cleared from her throat Alex in one fluid motion pulled the garrote, wrapped it around Marcus throat, pulled and twisted the lethal wire. The garrote was specially made for Alex and the steel wire was strong and as sharp as a razor. He had cut off Marcus head in one silent, swift motion. Blood gushed from the exposed neck. The head fell beside the sleeping girl. Marcus pulled out the vile of herbs from under the mattress opened it and poured the contents into Marcus half open mouth. The herbs were an ancient mix created by witches from the Carpathian Mountains to keep the living dead in their graves. Marcus body now began a rapidly transition from flesh into a skeleton.

Alex bit into the girl's neck and finished killing her by drinking the rest of her blood. He would let her family and the police try and figure out what happened to this girl. It will keep them busy for quite a while I should think thought Alex. Alex returned to his bat form, walked to the window sill and flew back to the penthouse terrace. He took a shower, got dressed, exited the building and took a cab back to his rv or bus, whatever these Americans wished to call it was fine with him. They seemed to have an abundance of names for about everything. He simply thought of it as a grave. He had been too tired to fly or run. The emotional energy needed for his interactions with Dell and Marcus had drained him. The blood of the virgin had been sweet but it was not enough to satiate his thirst.

The next night Dell received a call in his room. "It is done Dell. Come to my bus and I will instruct you on what to do and how to obtain my possessions." Dell got in his pickup and drove toward the trailer park. Dell was almost as nervous and scared as he had been when Alex had introduced himself. Dell was scared to show up and he was scared not to show up. He rationalized that if Alex wanted him dead he would be dead. Surely he wouldn't turn him into one of them, or would he? No where to run, no where to hide just like fucking Vietnam all over again. Before Dell could knock on the door Alex said thru a hidden speaker, "Come in, Dell." The room was very dark. Alex turned up the lights and motioned for Dell to have a seat.

"*Mr. Entertainment*, will no longer be a problem. I'm tired. I don't want to give lengthly explanations so let us get to it Mr. Hicks. Here is a business card. The name, address and contact information of my business agent is on there. He has all of the contracts for you to sign. Tell him nothing. I told him he is paid well to obey and not ask questions and to settle his curiosity I told him I was dying of cancer and was going to a private resort to die privately and I had given you my wealth before I died. The why was a private affair between us; with the commission this man is making he and his family are set for eternity. By tomorrow you will be one of the wealthiest men on earth. Let us now have no drama. I will tell you what to do. Just do it." Tomorrow I will leave the door to the bus unlocked. I will be lying on the bed asleep. There will be an axe by the bed. Take that axe and chop off my head. Strike hard and often until my head is completely severed. There will be no body to worry about. There will be a cup by my bed with herbs in it. After my head is removed stuff those herbs into my open mouth. I can't emphasize this enough to put the herbs in my open mouth. It is as important as the physical act of severing my head. I am so old I will quickly turn to dust. I would think a vacuum cleaner sufficient to clean up my remains. There has to be a joke in there somewhere doesn't there. Now go."

Dell did what he was told. It took three good strikes before the head fell completely off and true to his instructions Dell poured the herbs from the cup by the bed into the open mouth. almost immediately the corpse turned into dust. Dell found a vacuum in the closet and cleaned up the mess. Dell went outside and emptied the vacuum cleaner bag into the wind. He also needed to make sure the rv was completely unhooked from the electricity, sewer and water. Dell walked over to his old pickup, threw the keys in the front seat and returned to the bus. Dell went back inside the huge rv, walked to the front, sat in the driver's seat, started the engine and headed for home. "See I told you Red it was a bus not an rv or a motor home. Even old Alex called it a bus."

The End

The Ballad of Lester Hill

It has been said that if a man enjoys what he does to earn a living he never works a day in his life. Lester Hill not only enjoyed his work he loved it. Lester Hill had never worked a day in his life, figuratively and literally. Lester Hill's job was to test the new batches of fentanyl and lactose cut heroin his contact had mixed with pure guesswork on his kitchen table. If Lester didn't die and gave a positive nod his supplier would later bring him a baggie full of individually wrapped paper grams of the batch Lester had just survived from. If Lester survived the hit of heroin as an added incentive to keep up the good work an ounce of primo pot was left for Lester's personal consumption.

Lester was in Lester Heaven. He got high, read his books and magazines, watched tv, movies and dreamed. His two associates, Big Moo and Little Moo, shared the apartment where Lester ran his ghetto empire. They would anxiously watch to see if Lester survived the sample so they could help Lester smoke up the pot the dealer had left. Lester's associates did the actual work of dealing the heroin on the corner as Lester dreamed of better things to come. Before turning over the heroin to his cronies Lester would take the slightest amount from each paper gram replacing what he had taken with the appropriate amount of baking soda. Lester's two roommates were a pair of very unique individuals to say the least.

Big Moo was huge, as big as a small water buffalo and almost as smart as one. He was proud of the fact that he had waited until middle school to drop out and could both read and write and was not a dumb ass like his little brother, Little Moo who stopped going to school in the fifth grade. Little Moo could read comics, his favorite and print his name. "Fuck the rest of that Honky shit.", was all Little Moo ever said on the subject of education. Little Moo was not quite as big as Big Moo but almost. He was as big as say a juvenile water buffalo instead of a full sized adult. Both were handy to have around if one were in the drug business was Lester's thinking on the subject.

The brothers had given themselves the pseudonyms of Big Moo and Little Moo after Big Moo had read parts of one of Lester's books, **"The Mau Mau Uprising in Kenya",** by Sir Richard Little, M.B. E., aloud to his little brother. During the length of the recital the older of the two brothers had constantly mispronounced the name of the Mau Mau, (which rhymes with Wow Wow), Rebellion as the Moo Moo Rebellion. After the reading the consensus of the two dimwits was, "those African niggers were bad ass", and to honor the bad assness of those in the homeland and to show their solidarity with Mother Africa they would from then on be known as Big Moo and Little Moo. Most of their friends just thought they were having a bit of fun with their size. Both were the size of a large cow. Fuck it. You big bastards call yourself whatever you want was the general feeling in the neighborhood. Who was going to argue with the giant brothers.

Lester was in the middle of one of his favorite fantasies as he lay stoned on his couch his mind being consumed by the dreams induced by the latest batch of heroin. He would help smoke the pot the brothers were cramming into the bong. It would put a nice edge on things. This particular heroin induced fantasy was the one where he, Lester was the Drug Kingpin of the whole city. In Lester's drug induced euphoria he was indeed on his way up, a cool ass kicker with good looking ho's, and plenty of cash to throw around the clubs on champagne. Nobody messed with Lester if they wanted to stay alive. Lester had repeated this same fantasy for about fifteen years more or less between his stints in and out of prison. In the fantasy the ho's and bitch's were always different and the clubs would be the new, latest and coolest place to be. Lester varied his violence in fantasy from maybe just kicking one guy's ass to kicking a whole bunch of ass. In the real world the only thing that changed for Lester was the potency of the heroin and the couch he would be lying on.

Lester Rides Again

The last time Lester had been in prison he had told the shrink, "I only fucks the men when I'm in here. I like the bitches when I'm in the world. I ain't no homo."

Lester had lived with at least nine different desperate and lonely women since his last release from incarceration but all had kicked him out when they finally realized what a worthless walking bag of shit he really was. Lester liked to live with women on welfare so they could pay for everything, feed him and fuck him. This lifestyle provided Lester the life he desired, a life of lying around and living in the fantasies of his dreams. He insisted all of the women help support his lifestyle by letting him deal heroin and pot from their apartments. Five in the group threw him out because they got tired of the buggery. It seemed Lester liked to fuck them in their poop shoot when they were sleeping. The other four were junkies too and Lester would jump their poop shoots when they were passed out on his dope. Not one of the four figured out why their butt holes hurt so much every morning. They all thought the pain was from the constant constipation brought on by the opiates, These four eventually ran him off too because he ate too much of their kids food and wouldn't help pay the bills. Good citizen Lester stole money from all of them to buy copies of his favorite magazines, **Big Un's** and **Knockers.**

Lester was an avid reader. He often stole books and magazines from the public library. He wished the library would get subscriptions to his two favorite magazines. Maybe he would put a request for **Big Un's** and **Knockers i**n the suggestion box. Magazines full of photos of large breasted women were not to be had at the library. "Cheap bastards.", thought Lester. Lester was a titty man. Lester never told the shrink at the joint his number one fantasy was to have a pair of huge boobs himself. If he had a pair of giant hooters he could become the defacto *Queen* of the cell block if not the whole prison. If he had a pair of big tits he would never want for drugs or commissary again. If he got lucky one of the gang leaders would make him his bitch and then nobody would mess with him. Lester kept this particular fantasy buried deep, very deep only to be brought out when alone with copies of his favorite magazines and a really good shot of dope.

Meanwhile back at the ranch, Lester came down from his dream state of the heroin to where he could function and told the Moo brothers to not smoke all of his pot while he went to the library to score some new reading material. Lester brought back one book, a novel and three magazines. He had put all three in the front of his pants and calmly walked out of the library. One of the magazines was the latest issue of **Time**. Unknown to Lester there was an article in the magazine that after Lester read it would fire his imagination to new heights. His wildest fantasy was now possible. The article was about the liberal governor of his state. The good governor had just passed a law where inmates in the state prisons could now get tax payer paid hormones, breast implants and sex change operations. Lester was so excited he took another shot of the heroin to calm his nerves and then helped the brothers smoke a couple of bowls to take the edge off of the heroin. He wanted those tax payer tits and was willing to do anything to get him a pair.

Lester could see his future clearly in his opiated haze. It was as clear as day. All he had to do was return to prison and convince the shrink he was a candidate for free implants.The shrink would be easy. He was a government worker and all he cared about was his full benefit retirement; in order to have as few problems as possible he pretty much went along with whatever the inmates wanted.

Happy inmates didn't riot and take hostages. Lester's dream could become a reality. He could become the "*Queen of the Joint*". Lester needed to commit a crime so he could go back to the can. It had to be the right crime. Twenty-five to life would be the best scenario. His state didn't execute criminals anymore so life in prison was one possibility. Lester had second thoughts about life in prison. The lifers in max could be dangerous. Max sucked because those men had nothing to lose. They might kill you on a whim. Maybe it would be best to get caught dealing or robbing and get maybe twenty to thirty years. Lester needed to smoke a couple of more bowls in the bong to clear his mind and give his choice of crimes some more thought. Lester didn't want to get his ass killed in prison just the benefits of prison life. Lester loved prison.

He could wear his pants low there and get all the sex he wanted. He was fed three meals a day, healthcare, commissary, a warm bed, clothes, a library, tv and all the drugs he wanted. If he got those free tits the drugs and commissary would come rolling in with his male prostitution. It was a win, win. For Lester going to prison and getting a pair of government tits was like winning the lottery. Lester would literally be living in a whorehouse that offered a free buffet, a buffet of food and drugs. The Moo brothers wouldn't be a problem. He might use them to help him get busted but he didn't want their company in the joint. He didn't want anyone on the inside who had known him on the outside. These were two different worlds needed to stay separate. It only complicated matters to have people around you in the joint that knew you on the outside. Now Lester needed a plan.

The Last Rodeo of Lester Hill

With Lester's rap sheet going back to prison was simply the formality of getting caught red handed committing a crime. Lester took a hit of dope and dreamed his Crime Lord dream. In this dream he was James Cagney, Humphrey Bogart, Sam Jackson and Denzel all rolled into one. He went into banks and drug dens with guns blazing. No one dare fuck with, *the Lester.*

Lester came down, walked over to his closet and found what he was looking for: an old shoe box, a broken alarm clock, some assorted wires from stolen cd players, and a can of red spray paint left over from his graffiti artist period. To complete his plan he walked into the kitchen and found an empty paper towel roll in the trash which he immediately spray painted red. As soon as the paint dried Lester put all of the assorted pieces in the shoe box then sat down and scribbled a note on a piece of cardboard torn from a cereal box. Lester admired his word craft and left the note on the top of the shoe box. The note said, *There is a bomb in the box. If you want to live give me all of the money in the drawer.* All of the work gathering supplies and writing the note tired Lester. He need a break. The bank could wait until tomorrow. Lester needed another hit to settle his nerves.

Lester woke up somewhere around noon the next day, shot up just a taste of heroin, smoked a bowl and walked the three blocks to the bank branch closest to his apartment. Lester took no precautions. the whole idea was to get caught. Lester was made sure to smile at all the cameras in the bank to help identity him to the police. Lester put the box next to the teller window, handed the teller the note, opened the shoe box to show her the contents, smiled and said, "Good Morning Miss. Please help me with this withdrawal." The clerk read the note, her face changed from the smiling, friendly one moments ago to a look of fear then almost instantaneously back to smiling when she saw the assortment of junk in the shoe box. "This guy is desperate.", she thought to herself.

The clerks were trained to cooperate fully with all robberies. She pushed the silent alarm with her foot, emptied her drawer of bills and stacked the bills neatly under the plexiglass window in front of her. In his haste to get going Lester had forgotten to bring a bag to put the money in. His first instinct was to empty the shoe box contents and put the money in but people might notice a black man emptying a shoe box of trash on a bank floor so he politely asked the clerk, "Mam, do you have a garbage bag or a money bag or something I can put this money in?"

"Yes sir, just a moment and I'll give you my trash bag right here under the counter." She bent over, took the empty garbage bag from the trash can and handed it to Lester.

Instead of reaching for the bag Lester said to the teller, "Ma'm would you mind putting the money in that bag and then I'll be leaving?"

"Yes sir,", the clerk scooped the bills into the plastic bag. "Thank you sir. have a nice day." If anyone noticed the activities at the window they pretended not to. Lester walked leisurely out of the bank toward his apartment whistling a little tune as he walked. Lester went straight to his apartment. The Moo brothers were no where to be seen. Lester took an extra big hit of dope and waited for the inevitable. The cops weren't too long in playing their part in Lester's choreographed drama by busting in Lester's door and hauling his stoned ass off to jail. The over worked inept free government lawyer played his part to the hilt. Lester's plea deal couldn't have been better if Lester had sentenced himself. Lester was going home. His real home, the state pen for a minimum of twenty years and a maximum not to exceed thirty-five years.

Lester knew the drill of prison so well he could do it in his sleep. As soon as he got settled in to his new cell he made his appointment with the good prison shrink, Dr. Peabody. Lester pleaded his case, the good doctor feigned interest, scribbled a few notes in Lester's file and scheduled him for female hormone shots to be provided free by the good citizens of Lester's state. Dr. Peabody scheduled a series of appointments with Lester to assess his progress of turning into a woman with balls. Lester used every appointment to further his argument for his boob job.

Finally after three years of bullshit Lester got his wish. His new huge tits were a tremendous success among the general population of the prison. His regular clients were ecstatic; with Lester's new clients the favors would now start rolling in. Lester would have to up his rates. Tits were a valuable commodity in a prison full of horny men. As soon as Lester recovered he made sure his tits were seen by as many inmates as possible. Lester made sure to flirt often with the leader of the largest prison gang at every opportunity. His flirtations bore fruit and soon he was the private property of El Negro, the leader of the notorious prison gang, F.Y.M. (Fuck Your Mama).

Lester's prison world changed. His dream had come true. He was the absolute, *Queen of the Prison*. No one dared mess with him under the protection of his Prince Charming, El Negro. His favors were now the exclusive property of El Negro. For his services Lester not only received a sore asshole from El Negro's huge cock but first access to the best drugs coming in to the prison. Lester was in love. He loved his life, his new tits and his criminal lover. Lester's world was about to come crashing down. His lover boy got paroled and as a parting gift left his bitch, Lester to his gang as a reward for their loyalty Lester had not been told about his new status by El Negro.

Lester was invited to a private party in the kitchen where a batch of primo raisin wine was brewing. The gang brought an ounce of coke that had been smuggled in that day. They stripped Lester an made him give all of them a blow job before bending him over a cauldron used for mashing potatoes and repeatedly raping him while snorting coke and drinking the home made wine. The gang left a bleeding Lester on the floor of the kitchen. No one had to remind him to keep his mouth shut. They had torn Lester's anus so bad it required several surgeries to repair. Lester's butt fucking days were over for a while. As soon as Lester butt hole was healed enough he was transferred to a different prison.

Lester was determined to not let his beautiful tits go to waste at his new home so he set up a pay as you play plan to let the inmates enjoy them. Lester was still able to give blow jobs so he was still in business just a no go up the poop shoot business for a while. Lester didn't like to give blowjobs. Queers and homos gave blowjobs and

Lester had made it clear he wan't either. Lester believed he was something special, a sort of half man, half woman hybrid. What a fucking idiot! Lester had explained his thoughts to the shrink. A man/girl/thing still has to live thought Lester so he would just have to suck it up and give head for a while. I made a joke thought Lester. Suck it up, blowjobs, get it. Now that was funny in Lester's warped thinking.

Lester was doing good. He was happy at least until a gang member from F.Y.M. was transferred to his prison and claimed his ownership of Lester. This pissed off the other inmates who considered Lester their property. This argument over the affections of Lester the man/woman/it prisoner caused the biggest riot this prison had ever seen.

It was on. Shanks of all descriptions stabbed away. Anything not tied down was thrown at inmates and guards. Fires were started, toilets were plugged. Finally the warden gave the go ahead and the tear gas canisters were launched and the shot guns came out. The inmates tried to take a school teacher hostage. The warden sent in his elite rescue team and they shot and killed several inmates in the school while rescuing the terrified teacher. The last step that brought the riot to a screeching halt was when the warden gave the tower guards permission to shoot anyone in the yard engaging in any act of violence. Two inmates were wounded and one killed before the whole yard dropped on the ground to signal the fight was over. The prison was put on lockdown. The warden was put on administrative leave for over reacting. The prison system paid over twenty million dollars settling law suits for violating the prisoners' rights.

Lester was fucked, not butt fucked just the plain old put in a bad situation kind of fucked. During lockdown every inmate was restricted to his cell and fed from paper bags. All Lester could no was lay here and play with his tits. Lester was no homo as he had previously stated on more than one occasion but he sure could use some company. As the lockdown continued Lester became even more depressed. Finally after a year of being locked down and no end in sight Lester gave his tits one last glance in the mirror and strangled himself to death by choking himself with a sheet tied to an upper bunk which he jumped off of. He struggled trying to free himself but it was too late. His feet became tangled in the sheet and he could not for all of his efforts gain his footing.

Lester's body was found and sent to the prison morgue for an autopsy where they removed Lester's implants before burying him. Implants can be reused. The removal and reuse of implants was part of the new cost cutting plan implemented by the new warden.

I read somewhere that angels had no sex organs. I guess Lester will have to fly around tit less. At least the other angels won't think he's a homo!

The End

The Dementia Files

Part I

Letters to Micki

Dear MIcki,   21 June 2021

I was so sorry to hear of the death of your husband, Alfred. I know these are difficult times for you. I just went thru the same thing when my dear, sweet Suzi passed away. Let me back up for a moment and remind you who I am.

Fifty-six years ago I was your neighbor on Kentucky Ave. in Sheffield. We were engaged to be married when I left for Vietnam. Ring any bells? Remember me now? I kept track of you all of these years thru a mutual friend of ours, Ken Burns. He told me about your loss.

I would love to hear from you. I got your phone number and address from the internet. I tried calling you several times but it rang and rang and no one ever answered so I decided to drop you a line.

I won't waste anymore of your time. I would love to hear from you and if possible see you again. My phone number is 870-555-7659.

Your old friend,

Gary Fellows
805 Cedar Creek Road
Brockwell, Arkansas   72557

Two weeks later.........

Dear Gary,

Of course I remember you silly. How could I forget my first love? I lost my phone. Calling me for now is a waste of time until I can find it. It has been tough since Alfred passed but I'm making it. He was the love of my life and I miss him terribly. I'm sorry you lost your wife. Grief is hard isn't it?

What have you been up to all of these years? I haven't heard anything about you for years. Write me and tell me about your life and what you are up to.

Love,
Micki

As soon as I read her letter.......

Dear MIcki,   9 July 2021

Hard to believe we are such oldsters and still kicking isn't it. I know that at least half of our graduating class has passed away. I'll try and catch you up on what I was doing all of those years since I saw you last. I'll only hit the high spots, some of the hard times I would just as soon forget.

I'll be honest when I got the *Dear John* letter from you I was really hurt. It was even harder knowing you left me for Tommy. I bet he couldn't wait for me to get gone. I guess it takes two to tango. I'll never forgive that bastard. That's the past but at the time it really messed me up. Thank God for my buddies over there, they helped me get thru it and move on. I am hoping we can be completely honest with each other. I believe that is the best way.

When I cam back from Vietnam I tried to reconnect with my old friends in Alabama but they seemed like a bunch of kids to me. I had a taste of the real world outside of Alabama and I liked it. My old friends acted just like they did in high school. I could only relate to other veterans I crossed paths with. I started hanging with Billy who you also knew. He had been a Lurp over there. A very dangerous job. We both made pals with an ex Marine we ran across by the name of John. We three became best friends.

We tried our best to drink all the beer and chase all the girls in Alabama. I attended college to study law but after one semester I thought to hell with this and stuck out my thumb and headed West. I always wanted to see the West.

I fist headed to Tucson, Arizona. I worked any and all jobs I could find. I got itchy feet and rode a motorcycle I had purchased to California to visit friends I had made in the military. I wound up in Northern California working in a sawmill. I crashed my motorcycle, stuck out my thumb and made it all the way to Alaska. It was getting cold up there and I couldn't find a job so I took what money I had and got a ferry boat back to the states.

I hitched and worked my way to Wyoming where I worked on a few ranches working with cattle and horses. I migrated to Texas where I wound up working in the oil fields. This was a life changing experience for me. It turns out I have a natural ability with math. I was trained as a surveyor and later a navigator in the oil exploration business. I traveled all over for years doing this work on land and sea. I met my Suzi when working in the oil business.

We were married and decided if we wanted a family we needed to settle down. We settled down in Midland, Texas. We were married for forty-three years. We raised three good kids. I now have three grand kids.

Here is perhaps the biggest shock of all. While in Midland I went back to college and got a degree in math and became a school teacher. Can you believe it, me of all people a school teacher! I retired as a teacher and we moved to Arkansas where Suzi had family. She got sick and passed away there.

I guess I did not lead a conventional life but looking back I have no regrets. We all move along doing the best we can.

Enough about me. What about you? What have you been up to all of these years? Remember we are too old to bullshit each other.

Love,
Gary

P.S. I would really like to see you again if you want.

Three weeks later..........

Dear Gary,

Sorry it has taken so long for me to answer. My son bought me another phone but I have already lost it. My son took my car away so I am stranded at home unless someone comes by which is not too often.

It sounds like you have had an interesting life after leaving here. You a school teacher is hard to imagine. You were always so wild and hated school if I remember. Here's a flash for you, I was a teacher too. How strange both of us being school teachers.

I'll be honest with you too. I learned a long time ago that honesty is always the best policy. Tommy and I lasted only a few months before we split up. I remarried another boy from our high school, Billy Franks. If you remember him. He turned into an abusive drunk. I left him and took our son with me. I married one more local drunk named Tom Lawson. He was rich and owned a store but he was just another drunk. I had my fill of Alabama and drunken husbands so I took a teaching job in Alaska where I met Alfred. He was kind and not a drunk. He worked at a radar station near the school I taught at. We were so happy together.

We both retired to Alabama where Alfred died of cancer. I would love to see you again. If you are ever down this way come by my home.

Love,
Micki

One week later.........

There I was knocking on her door. She was so desperate for human companionship she insisted I stay in her guest bedroom. I was shocked by her looks. She looked basically the same as when I last saw her. She was as lonely as I was. Two days later she told me she had been diagnosed with dementia. I detected something was not quite right with her but I didn't know what until she confided her diagnosis to me. Some things she was doing were obvious, others not so much. I decided right then and there to start a diary of my time left with my first and possibly my last love, Micki.

Part II

Dementia Diary

Day 3

I told her today my true feelings that I loved her, had always loved her and all of those years we were separated I always asked about her when I heard from old friends in Alabama. Tonight we started sleeping together. We didn't get much sleep. Her damn dog even got in on the action. The little bastard was licking my balls. I put his ass out the door. Later that night must have been about 3 or 4 in the morning Micki got up to piss. She stood in the doorway and instead of just coming straight back to the bed is staring at me and says, "Who are you?" My first thought was to get the hell out of there. This woman is nuts. Thank God I remembered her dementia. I reminded her who I was and that she invited me to stay. I almost packed my bag and went home. This was just too bizarre. She finally came back to bed and went to sleep. I lay there for a while debating on whether to pack my shit and git or stay.

Day 4

Everything back to normal. I went into the bedroom and sniffed the bed. Something really stank in her bed. I took off the sheets. The mattress was covered in dog piss stains. I changed the sheets and put the ones on the bed in the washer. That night the smell was still there. It was coming from Micki. I realized she had not taken a bath or a shower or changed clothes in the 4 days I had been there. We are very passionate toward each other. A wildness I didn't realize old farts like us were still capable of. It wasn't just me. She was as wild as I was.

Day 5

She woke me up in the middle of the night for snoring. She told me I had to leave. I went to the other bedroom and went to sleep. She screamed at me "Go back to your apartment. Your snoring is keeping me awake." I don't have an apartment. I'm not driving 6 hours to Arkansas in the middle of the night. I closed the door and went back to sleep. I didn't hear another peep until we woke up around noon. She looked at me and I swear said, "Why didn't you sleep with me last night?" I told her she ran me off. She denied doing it. WTF

Day 6

God damn. She is nutty as a squirrel turd. It's 3 in the morning and I'm driving home to Arkansas. After we screwed until we were both exhausted we both fell asleep. She woke me up in the middle of the night and said, "you have to leave or I'm calling the police." She's so fucking nuts. I'd rather drive home then deal with the cops. God only knows what she would tell them. Fucking Nut!

Day 7

I'm in fucking Arkansa. I called her on her land line phone she doesn't even remember having. I let it ring until she answers. She doesn't remember a damn thing. I got the number of her wall phone from her son. She wants to know why I left. Asked me when I'm coming back. I must be crazy but here I go again. Driving back tomorrow.

Day 8 and 9

I'm back in Alabama. She's acting like we haven't seen each other in years. Wants to know if I'm staying. I unpack and wish myself good luck. We pick up where we left off. As soon as the sex is over I go to the guest room to sleep. She comes in and starts another session that last util dawn. I swear this woman makes me feel like a kid again. I love her crazy or not.

Day 10

She has been feeding that fucking dog of hers out of the same bowls we eat out of. I watched after feeding the dog she rinsed the dish out in cold water then ate a bowl of cereal out of it. I told her that was nasty and if she didn't stop I I was going to throw the fucking dishes away. She didn't stop so I threw the dishes in the trash. I went to the dollar store and bought the dog a bowl and us paper plates, styrofoam bowls and plastic drinking cups. If she noticed she didn't say a word, just carried on as normal. Another word about DooDoo her dog. She feeds the little bastard everything she eats including sweets. He rewards her by shitting and pissing all over the house. I'm not touching it. She can clean up after it. Not me.

Day 11

She spends her days working in her yard. She hates housework and likes yard work. I hate working in yards. I think it's a waste of resources. I like to cook so I take care of the inside, she takes care of the outside. My cooking is putting some meat on her bones. When I came down she was as skinny as a rail living on frozen meals and junk food. I shop for us now. Before I got here her son came by every couple of weeks and filled her freezer and food pantry. She can't go to the store by herself. She can't find her way back home. Forgets where she is. She still tries to find stores and business that have been closed for twenty years.

Day 12

Out of the blue tonight she tells me after sex to "Leave because she needs to sleep.". I explain it's a 6 hour drive home. She just stares and says again, "You need to leave. I need to go to sleep.". I don't know who is crazier her or me for putting up with this shit. Off again to Arkansas.

Day 13 and 14

God Damn. I'm still mad. She doesn't remember anything. I tell her I'm not a yoyo every time she wants to be alone I can't drive 6 hours. I also tell her to take a shower. I love her but she's getting pretty ripe. When I get back when she undresses for bed I'm going to take her filthy clothes and put them in the washer. Her panties have enough shit in them to use them for fertilizer. Why is this woman so fucking dirty? Her son says it's those fucking Eskimos she taught in Alaska. Water was scarce so baths were a luxury until warm weather. It's fucking hot in Alabama. All the faucets work fine. Damn.

Day 15

I'm back. She almost burned the house down while I was gone. She left a pot on the stove and forgot it was there. She has already done this once with the oven. She told me today she loves me. I asked her if she was sure she knew who I even was. Sometimes she calls me Alfred.

Day 16

She lost the tv remote today. I found it in the yard where she was weeding. I guess if she got tired of weeding she could change channels. If you can figure her out let me know will you.

Day 17

She is watching tv on the microwave. She put in a frozen meal, picked up an old tv remote that doesn't work and tried to change channels on the microwave. She thought she was watching a cooking show. Her fucking dog is having seizures. He was doing a Michael Jackson moonwalk backwards. I'll take him to the vet tomorrow.

Day 18 and 19

The vet put him on anti-seizure meds which means I'll have to give them to him. I decide traveling might be a good idea. She won't go without DooDoo. I take her to Hot Springs, Arkansas. I give the dog his meds but refuse to clean up after him. She forgets to take him out so he craps and pisses in the room. I bought her a new bathing suit, a beautiful full bathing suit. Micki still has a beautiful young woman's body so the suit looks good on her except for one itty, bittty detail that never entered my mind. When she steps out into the public area of the hot pools at first glance she looks very nice until I saw those two huge wads of hair sticking out of the crotch of her bathing suit. I'm a guy, shaving a snatch never entered my mind. I thought girls took care of all of that kind of stuff. I'm embarrassed for her. It looks like someone painted two big black lines on the inside of her legs. It is pubic hair, giant wads of black pubic hair. I rush over and cover her with a towel. I don't think she even noticed. She still got in the pools. I cover her up when she gets in and out. I started calling her Chubaccca.

Day 20

I thought it would be a good idea to stop at my cabin and spend a few days before going to Alabama. She thought we were at her grandparents cabin that had been torn down twenty years ago. She kept insisting we were at a lake in Alabama that was drained at the same time the cabin disappeared. I finally convinced her it was not her grandfather's cabin but she insisted she was at a lake in

Alabama, She decide it was getting late and she wanted to go home. I explained I wasn't going to drive 6 hours this late. She cussed me out grabbed her dog and her suit case, walked to the edge of the driveway and turned around. She said she was going to walk home but got scared of the dark.

Day 21

Today after cursing me out she walked off to I didn't know where. I drove the main roads before going to the sheriff's office to get some help. She was sitting there. She had gotten lost and didn't have a clue where she was and after crossing a field had sat down in someone's yard. The home owners saw her and asked her what she was doing there. She didn't have a clue. They called the sheriff and they picked her up and were waiting for someone to come and claim her. Never a dull moment.

Day 22

Still no shower. She really stinks. I got so fed up I pushed her out of the bed with my foot and made her sleep on the couch. Still no shower her only response was to cuss me out. She really gave me a cussing out later that day when I was trying to force a seizure pill down DooDoo's throat. I turned the duty over to her. DooDoo never got another pill. She would feed him ice cream, candy, chips or whatever she was snacking on. He would seize up and she would pick him up and pet him. She tried to feed him in my dishes. I threw them away and went and bought another set of doggie bowls and paper plates.

Day 23

We are back in Alabama. I have to take her to her neurologist for her once a year visit. What a fucking joke. Dr. Shitbird just sits there and does't say a word. You tell her what is going on. You leave. Good news. DooDoo died. What a pain in the ass. No more pets for her at least while I'm around. She can't take care of herself much less a fucking dog. I assure the doctor she gets all of her meds. I inherited that job of making sure she takes her meds and at the right time. When I got here she was taking them whenever she felt like it. Not good.

Day 24

Decided to try a longer trip. Going to Las Vegas, via Amarillo, Taos and Winslow. The band U2 is playing at the Las Vegas Sphere. I am fascinated by that place and really want to see U2 in concert there. Amarillo was interesting. We stayed at the Big Tex motel and restaurant. She got mad at me because the room was not to her perfect temperature specifications. She was going to the motel office which was right next door to demand her own room but instead went into the restaurant and demanded the room form the hostess. She was barefooted which added to the fun. I had to go retrieve her by which time she forgot why she was there.

Day 25

Taos was fun. She only cursed me out once in public right on Taos Plaza. She insisted on going shopping alone which was impossible. That night when we went out to dinner she announced she had lost her credit card. We were sharing expenses so this was no small event. I really got mad over her carelessness. She cursed me like a dog and demanded to go home. I drove her to the Albuquerque airport and escorted her to the airline counter where she tried to buy a ticket to Alaska with her medical card. I had second thoughts about letting her go anywhere alone and drove us all the way back to Taos where she magically found her card in her luggage. It seems she thought I was a thief and hid her card. She is driving me mad arguing with her every time it is her turn to use her card. If I could afford it I would tell her to shove her card up her ass.

Day 25

Stopped in Winslow. It's the town made famous by that Eagle's song. There is a local cafe there that is worth the trip just to eat there. They built some statues of the Eagles downtown and now the tourist flock there to have their pictures taken by them.

Day 26

Made it to Vegas. Left her in our room all day. Every time I came to see if she wanted to go somewhere she would curse me out so I would walk out and go do something. I stayed drunk the whole time out of necessity. I was so drunk by the time dinner rolled around I fell out of my chair in the fancy restaurant.

Day 27

Got a limo to the concert. I am really wasted. I begged her all day not to take her large bag to the concert. Security of course took it. I tried to stand up for her but to no avail. My old man's bladder made me piss about every ten minutes the whole concert which made everybody sitting around us mad. Sorry. Your days are coming amigo. She acted good. I was the fuck up.

Day 28 thru Day 32

We came back thru Texas. I love Texas. I lived there 45 years. She left her card at different places at least three tines. I had to start watching her transactions to make sure she got her card back before leaving; For this I got cursed out in gas stations and cafes across the whole state. She tried to hide her card one more time but I was on to her and found it.

Day 33

In the last month she has taken a total of three showers. She has changed clothes more often... it must be Alabama etiquette while traveling, just cover the dirt. I don't even argue anymore with her about cleanliness. Arguing accomplishes nothing. All she ever says besides calling me every name in the book is, "You don't know me,' whatever the fuck that means.

Day 34

She asked me today if her parents left while she was working in the yard. She wanted to say good by before they left. That's nice. Her parents have only been dead for ten years!

Day 35

TV remote gone again. Finally found it on top of the lawn mower. Silly me I should have looked there first. She has been cursing me out all day for basically nothing.

Day 36

Still cursing me out for all offenses real or imagined. Her son suggest I take her to the doctor for a UTI test and get her some antibiotics. Because she refuses to bathe she gets a lot of UTI's. The first sign of a UTI with her is she gets mean and will curse me out for nothing. Good to know. I wonder if they have antibiotic IV's I can move around with her. If not I hope they will give me plenty of refills on her antibiotics. She is the filthiest human being I have ever known.

Day 37

Took her to the doc's. Yep. UTI. Wish he would prescribe a fucking bath. I would make her but I'm afraid she might get hurt then I'm in a whole new world of shit.

Day 38 thru Day 44

The antibiotics worked. She is back to her old crazy self.

Day 45

Drove to the beach in Florida today. She took a shower. I didn't say a word. I think 'll make it a holiday. We were going out to eat and when she came out of the bathroom instead of walking out the front door she walked into the closet and shut the door behind her. I waited until she figured it out and came out of the closet.

Day 46

I got another good cussing out today because I wouldn't take her out the moment she wanted to go. She announced she, "didn't need me", and walked out the door. I finished watching the ball game and decided I had better go find her. I opened the door and she was standing there where she had been the whole time. She had forgotten where she was and was too scared to go anywhere and had stood by the door to our room.

Day 47

Back home again. Temperature seems to be her main enemy. She can't ever seem to get it right. At home it's no problem. She keeps the heat on all summer. Yep, you heard me right. The heat on in summer. If she gets hot during the day she turns on a floor fan. She has central air conditioning. You have to go outside in the 95 degree heat to cool off. She goes to bed early so I turn the ac on at night or I couldn't sleep. During the day I just stay gone all day. We sleep until noon so I just have to go out during the afternoon. I go drink beer or workout. The movies are a nice escape.

Day 48

Good day today. She works outside. I bring back her something to eat. We watch tv only when I am there to turn it on and change channels. We are into a routine. Just the normal fuckups.

Day 49

Nothing new to report. She unplugged the tv when she went to bed. That's how she turns it off. This also kills the WIFI. I tried explaining it to her but she forgets. I finally made a big sign and hung it over where the tv plugs into the wall, DO NOT UNPLUG TV I WILL TURN THE TV OFF. It is working. Hurray!

Day 50
Pretty mild day. I stayed gone all day, She did mange to lose the gas cap to the lawnmower.

Day 51
We are pretty much into a routine. If things don't change I may sign off until there is some excitement.

Day 172
I'm proud to say we have had a most peaceful 4 months until today. Out of the blue she says, "Motherfucker these are not my pills." She then proceeds to go into my room and take my pills. "That's my pills dear."

"Motherfucker that's my pill dispenser."

"No dear. I bought that for $3 at the dollar store."

"That's mine motherfucker and you're just using it."

"Ok. Please take your pills."

"Those aren't mine."

Shit. I have to take her in for another UTI exam. She hasn't changed clothes or bathed in the last four months. Now she'e not taking her meds which means she will even be worse for a while.

Day 173
I took her to the clinic and yes it's a UTI. They started her on

antibiotics. They will take a few days to work so she will be bat shit crazy until she starts taking her meds again. I'm in for it.

Day174
She wants me to take her to her parents house. I say sure. Five minutes later she forgets. I leave. Her pills she is supposed to take for her memory are all over the house. I hid mine. I may change my name to Motherfucker. It's all she ever calls me when she gets like this. She says she has to get back to Alaska before school starts. She hasn't worked there in 15 years. I tell her the weeds are looking bad in the back yard and sneak out.

Day 175 tru 178
Just getting cussed out a lot. She is getting loopy not taking her dementia meds but If I try and talk to her I am once again "Motherfucker". She got to me once and I grabbed her and told her what was really going on. She fought back. Hit me a good one in the face. I took her to the ground and sat on her head until she agreed to calm down. Finally she did.

Day 179
She took her meds today just as quiet and normal as if nothing had happened. I told her what she had been doing and she looked at me and said as calm as could be, "I have to take my meds silly." The doctor also has given her a new dementia prescription. I have my fingers crossed.

Day 180

She spent a little time outside then the rest of the day watching tv. She has no interest in sex. She says she's too old. Funny two weeks ago she was all in.

Day 181

She just watches tv. I'm still the official channel guide and changer. Sleeps a lot which is good. I get to control the heater and ac. No sex.

Days 182 thru 185

Nothing to report. I cook, she eats. I turn on the tv, she watches it. She sleeps. Takes her meds. We kid around some. I talk. She listens. I think.

Day 186

I can't believe it but it's been almost a half of a year and I'm still here. If you could have known her when she was young it is hard to believe this is the same person. She has always been beautiful. She was so sweet and innocent. Life was so unfair to her. She finally met a decent man and he ups and dies. Then she gets dementia. So sad. I guess I was hoping I could get that girl back from my youth but that girl is gone lost in the fog of dementia.

Day 187

I need a break. I talk to her son about taking over her care. I'm going to my cabin for some R&R.

Day 188 thru 203

I'm at home. It sure is peaceful here in the mountains. I love to listen to the birds singing and the rain on the tin roof.

Day 204

I'm back. The fridge is full of frozen meals and soda. The cabinet is full of junk food. The tv remote is missing. I finally find it on the back porch. The tv is unplugged. She is lying in bed with a pile of books and photos. Her med dispenser looks like she has been taking them. Thank God for small miracles. The house is not 100 degrees. Hurray.

Day 205 thru 275

Repeat performance. Tv. Eat. Sleep Work in yard. Sex gone. No baths. I do take her out to eat sometimes. No one ever visits her.

Day 276

She's back. I got a good cussing out today. Apparently I'm not needed as her friends will be by to take her out. Strange coincidence I just mentioned her friends never come over. It's UTI time boys and girls. Back on antibiotics. I get so fed up I finally tell the doc about her filthiness. Her advice, "try to get her to bathe occasionally". Pure genius this one.

Day 277 thru 281

Mean as hell but takes her meds including antibiotics. Stinks to high heaven. I'm almost embarrassed to take her out anywhere.

Forget sex. Forgot to mention the holidays. Made it thru Christmas. I had to take her shopping at Walmart. She bought little kid gifts for her adult nephews and nieces. She bought dolls for her teenage granddaughter. A knife for her son. Her son came over and took the gifts with him and brought her a couple of presents wrapped up. She made me lug up a tree from the basement. She decorated it. I bought her a bathroom soap set as a hint. Hint not taken. I took the tree down the day after Christmas. Christmas is a big deal to her. For myself I dread it. I guess thats why I'm late mentioning it. My own family fell apart after my wife died. I never hear from my kids. I guess I'm not worthy of them. Who knows. I devoted my life to them. Ungrateful shits. My grandson does call every now and then. He and I were always close. I about raised the little guy. Enough about me. I'm whining. I hate whiners.

Day 282
Got the tv working. The routine is back. Funny isn't it when you get to a certain age and realize tomorrow is not guaranteed. You could die in your sleep and every day could be your last. I'm 75 and she is 73.

Day 283 thru 343
Peace in the valley. Two old people taking their meds, watching tv. We go out to eat. Sex is now what other people must do because we don't. I miss it. She doesn't. She did get up one day out of the blue and take a bath. I'm thinking about making it another holiday. I'm going to plan another vacation for us just to get out and about.

Day 343 thru 365
We drove to Gettysburg, Pa. and Washington. I've always wanted to see Gettysburg. It helped define our nation. We drove the entire battlefield.. I learned a lot. Washington was really something. We took in the sights on a tour bus. Walked thru the Smithsonian and the National Archives to see the Declaration of Independence and the Constitution. Went to the Air and Space Museum but it was closing. We did make the American Indian Museum which was having Eskimo dances. She got a kick out of that. She follows me like a shadow scared of getting lost.

Day 365
Can't believe it's been a whole year. I have talked to her family about putting her in a long term care facility where she can get proper care. They are receptive to the idea. Sometimes love is not enough. This poor woman needs professional care. I have done my best but I am old and tired. It would be different if we had spent a lifetime together as husband and wife but we didn't. She blames me for leaving her and I blame her for not waiting. I think after 56 years it might be time for me to move on. I'm signing off for now. Don't know when I'll be back if I will at all. I may pack my shit and git after all.

The End

The Frankenstein, Tarzan, Tonto Debates

"We are gathered here today to debate some of the key issues affecting our nation. As the Presidential election grows nearer, we here at Harvard will attempt to ask the tough questions. We have assembled a panel of the leading academics from the Ive League Universities on one side and to compete with these leading intellectuals we welcome the leading brain trust from California. I think we all are familiar with the work of Frankenstein, Tarzan and Tonto. They need no further introduction. Let us begin."

"Our first question is on the economy as so many of our poorer citizens are falling behind. They are going without meals or spending such a large amount on food now they are not spending money elsewhere causing businesses to close. Our question is: Was the economy better under exPresident Trump than under the Biden/ Harris administration? Which candidate will be the best choice for the future of America, Harris or Trump? By flipping a coin before the show the Ivy League gets to answer first."

"Thank You. Our Consensus is yes absolutely. This question

has two phases to exam. Pre Covid and Post Covid. Before Covid the economy was in good condition. There was high employment in both branches of the economy both blue and white collar jobs. Inflation was under control and the country and the economy were thriving. Covid of course put a screeching halt to those gains and made any data after this point mute. The government at this point infused great amounts of cash into the system trying to keep the economy going but it did little to offset the damage. Recovery never did bounce back under Biden/Harris. They increased the national debt to astronomical proportions. They started more economic controls over the private sector and tried to regulate the free markets. This had devastating effects on our economy. They tried to hide these facts as gains as the Covid mandates were lifted. To make a long answer short. Donald Trump was much better at economics than his replacements and will be a better choice for the future."

"Now for a response from the California brain trust. I understand that each of you wish to respond individually instead of a composite response. Is that correct gentleman?"

"Ugh."

"Umm."

"Good Kimosabe"

"Thank you gentlemen. We will assume that as a positive response. Mr. Frankenstein would you like to comment first?"

"Trump good. Biden bad. Movie boss say answer questions same, Trump Bad, Harris good. Movie boss think monster no brain. Frankenstein have good brain. Book is good. Monster read book."

"Right, and you Mr. Tarzan?"

"Umm. Jane say, Trump save jungle. Good Life for Jane and Boy."

"And you Mr. Tonto?"

"Yes Tarzan, Frankenstein. Trump save ranch. Harris no savvy ranch."

"Thank you gentlemen. the next question concerns the invasion of millions and millions of undocumented immigrants, many whom are criminals, spies and terrorist while others are just poor people looking for the American dream. Would our borders be more secure under Donald Trump then would be under a Harris term as President? Ivy League your response."

"Absolutely the borders were more secure under President Trump. He closed them only to legal immigrants. Biden and Harris have endangered our country under the guise of Democracy. The dangers are real. They constantly use data to say how safe the country is. This use of data reminds us of the use of data by Mr McNamara to continue the bombing of North Vietnam. Raw data is worth a grain of salt. It is the human element that is most important. The Democratic Party bought into the nonsense of Defund the Police then unleashed thousands of criminals upon our own citizens to murder, rape and rob at leisure. The same party in the so called sanctuary cities are handing out benefits to illegals faster than to our poor people citizens already there. Our question is this, If the stare governments can hand out the free cash, housing, food and health care like that why did they not do it for our citizens first? There is some mystery here for us as to motive. It looks like from the outside they are trying to destroy our own poor people. None of it makes any sense to us."

Thank you. Mr. Frankenstein your response please."

"Ugh. MMMM. Book is good."

"I believe that was your response to the first question. Would you care to elaborate?"

"ARRRGGGHHHH!, BOOK IS GOOD. BOOK IS GOOD!'

"All right sir, Please put the chair down and have a seat. What about you Tarzan?'

"Jane say Trump good. Keep many bad men from jungle. We not safe with Harris."

"Tonto your answer please."

"Bad men come Kimosabe. We get on trail. Find bad men. Too many bad men for Tonto to track.Talk to Great White Father. Trump good Great White Father."

"Let's move on to our final question shall we?"

"Was the world a safer place under President Trump than it is now and would be under a Harris administration? Ivy League your answer is?"

"Under President Trump the world was at peace. He understood business and politicians and knew how to handle them. He was trying to move the country forward away from the remnants of WWII. He told NATO as much and for the first time they were paying their bills to us. He refused to back Ukraine's admission to NATO to keep the peace. Biden/ Harris undid all of his work and went backwards to Post WW II thinking and backed Ukraine's membership into NATO. Putin would have left Ukraine alone but not anymore. He wanted to keep the Americans away from his borders. Our foolish leaders have played right into his hands. President Trump had frozen Iran's wealth so they could not afford to go nuclear. Biden/ Harris again not understanding the world gave Iran six hundred billion dollars which they immediately turned around and handed to Hamas and Hezbollah to attack Israel while they worked on their bomb. All of the deaths, killing and bombings lie on Biden/Harris front door. They both have shown they are incapable as world leaders and are in fact dangerous to the world. Ex-President Trump by far is the superior negotiator on the world stage."

"Thank you. California your response."

"Fire bad. Monster want kill bad people."

"Tarzan."

"Jane say Men with guns come. No good. Tarzan move Jane and Boy deep in jungle. Call on animal brothers to kill men with guns."

"And Tonto your answer please."

"Ranger, me go see Ranger. Get facts. Tonto scout Harris trail. No have fight with Trump only bad man Harris."

"Ok. One important fact there Tonto. Harris is a woman."

"Make joke. Squaw no Great White Father in Washington.. Ha. Next you tell Tonto squaw Indian and no like Lone Ranger You make big joke on Tonto."

"Sorry Tonto, no joke everything I said is true."

"Me leave now join tribe in Mexico. Ranger smart him come too."

"Oh my God. Tarzan has pulled his knife and is running out of the studio. Somebody please try and stop Frankenstein!"

"Uh. Arrrrrgh. Me find BAD WOMAN. Frankenstein angry. FIRE BAD! FIRE BAD"

"You heard it here first. The Ivy League representatives are running and hiding. Tarzan and Tonto have left the building and Frankenstein is tearing the studio apart looking for "Bad Woman.." I am signing off now. We hope these debates have helped clear the air for some of you undecided voters. Good night."

In the aftermath of last nights debates. Frankenstein, Tarzan and Tonto were all fired by there respective Hollywood studies. Frankenstein was later that night sedated with a tranquilizer gun.

Tarzan, Jane and Boy were seen running into the trees near Redwood City, California and Tonto was reported to have crossed the border at Tijuana headed south. The Lone Ranger could not be reached for comment. The Ivy League debate team returned to their prospective universities where they were all put on administrative leave for publicly displaying views contrary to their schools liberal philosophy of shut the fuck up and do what you're told if you want to keep your job.

The End

The Amazing Life of General Lucious Solanum Maximus

Neighbors

General Maximus was born into a Samnite family. His family patriarch could see the writing on the wall and betrayed his tribe to join forces with Rome in the Civil Wars that followed. These wars were fought to bring the entire Italian Peninsula and the Italian tribes under the domination of Rome. His family had gained notoriety as raising some of the best horses in the whole of Italy. They were immediately welcomed into the Roman Army as Equestrians with the rank of Knight. Full citizenship would follow. They were assured after victory citizenship would only be a formality. The Senate would back such a prestigious family after their call to Roman arms. Their ranking as Equestrian was just under the rank of Senator. The Equestrians were the calvary of the Roman Army. They would provide their own horses and arms. At his time in the history of Rome their army was a citizen army dedicated to the advancement of the Roman culture and civilization.

After Rome's victory in the Civil War the Maximus family was rewarded with Roman citizenship and thousands of acres of their neighbor's lands were added to their existing farm. To work these vast lands the family imported hundreds of slaves. The lucky slaves were given duties in and around the homes of the patriarch, Gaius Tiberius Maximus, Knight of Rome. and his extended family. Gaius hired some of the local farmers who had been displaced by the government in Rome to be tenant farmers on the same land they had once owned. These new tenant farmers were hired to provide management of the land and the slaves. Needless to say the Maximus family made a lot of enemies as they became the overlords of those who a short time ago had been their neighbors.

The family was riding high for a while until bad fortune befell them. A severe drought brought crop failure. Gaius couldn't pay his taxes to Rome. The crop failure was followed by a revolt of the starving slave population that reduced the once beautiful estate to ashes. The Maximus family's prize horses except for a few were killed, eaten or stolen. The family was forced to sell their property to rich money lenders in Rome who worked for the very same Senators that had given them the land. They had no choice but to move. The survival of the family and their status as knights forced them to move to Rome. They invested their money in property and small businesses and did quite well. This was the family Lucious was born into a middle class Equestrian urban family of Rome. Their few prize horses were now kept in a stable in the back of their home. They were not poor by any means.

The really rich in Rome were the Senators who lived on the

hills surrounding Rome. The Senators owned most of the rural farm land and the slaves that worked it. Lucious grew up in the image of his grandfather. He was riding horses from the time he could walk. He trained in the art of war, philosophy and the Greek culture as the same as all of the wealthy boys of his age. As soon as he was old enough he joined his calvary regiment when it was called on by the Senate to fight Rome's enemies. Lucious proved himself in battle, a fearless and smart fighter. He could tell where men were needed better than those in rank above him and Lucious was the first in the fight. He was rewarded for his abilities by being offered the hand of a Senator's daughter, Claudia Metellus. She was rich, beautiful and ambitious. They were a perfect pair. Even though it was an arranged marriage the couple soon fell in love and grew to respect each other.

Lucious took Claudia's dowery and bought a city block of apartments and another of rental properties used by small businesses. Lucious hired masons and carpenters to turn half of the apartments into one huge home for him and his new bride. The businesses were told they had three choices: either pay rent, sell him a percentage of their business or move. Lucious had a neighbor whom he had been on several campaigns with, Julius Caesar and his second wife Pompeai. In battle he thought Caesar one of the bravest men he had ever seen. Like Lucious, Caesar was a Knight of the middle class. Caesar and his wife owned several blocks of real estate near theirs and like Lucious and Claudia had converted one of the buildings into their home. Caesar was very popular in the neighborhood.

Lucious was happy with his life and his place in roman society. Caesar was not content. He was a very ambitious man. As he confided his political plans to Lucious, Lucious began to see the true genius of the man. Caesar was running for Quaestor, (the first rung of the Roman political ladder), and he didn't have enough money to bribe enough of the Senators so in a moment of political clarity he decided he didn't need to bribe the Senators. He only needed to bribe the tribal vote counters. This is exactly what he did and won by a landslide. It wasn't long after his winning the election Caesar and his wife moved to housing better suited to a young couple on the rise. Caesar never forgot his friend Lucious and would call on him several times in the coming years to join him in his pursuit of fame and glory.

Beauty Tips

Life was good for Lucious and Claudia. Lucious expanded his business holdings in the city. While Lucious was consumed with business and his duties as a knight Claudia held court for her friends in their huge home. When Lucious was gone training with the army or away fighting Claudia became quite the host for her girlfriends whose husbands were likewise in the pursuit of battle honors or business ventures. The ladies, drank wine, gossiped, shared beauty tips and tried to out do each other's fashions. Claudia liked to be the center of attention. She was very vain and paid attention to every detail of her wardrobe and her looks. She was very determined to keep her skin looking like that of a young girl. She believed a pure clean skin was the key to her beauty and her desirability.

A well trusted slave in Claudia's house seeking favor told her mistress that in her country there was a well known recipe that guaranteed a woman's skin would maintain the look and feel of her youth no matter what their age. She would reveal this secret to her if she would grant her freedom with a few coins in her pocket. It was not an easy recipe to fill but it worked. The women of means where she was from were known far and wide for their beauty. That part of the slave's story was true the rest she manufactured on the spot. Do you want the eternal skin of your youth? It is up to you. Claudia jumped at the chance. She freed the slave on the steps of the Senate house and gave her three gold coins for her journey home. What the woman told Claudia shocked her to her core!

Claudia could not make herself do what the woman had told her until one day when she noticed in a reflection a wrinkle on her forehead. She decided that wrinkle would not do. Lucious might think she was getting old and find a new, younger wife. She had not given him any children which only increased her fears. She decided right then and there no matter how distasteful to follow the recipe. She went to the slave market and paid a fortune for a young beautiful virgin slave girl. The girl was proved to Claudia's satisfaction to be a virgin after she groped the girls vagina. She took the girl home. Claudia then called on a man she knew who ran a wine bar in one of their rented business stalls. Lucious told her to go to this man if she ever had the need for discretion. The man could be trusted completely. He will keep his mouth shut. Don't try and barter with him, pay him what he asked. If it is exorbitant Lucious would deal with him when he returned. That night the man as Claudia requested called upon her at home.

They took the girl into the basement of the house. The man

spread her out and tied her hands and feet between two roof supports. He then tore the terrified girls clothes off. He said some soothing words to the girl and as quick as lightening cut her tongue out and shoved it in her throat. He then methodically skinned her alive before bleeding her out into a ceramic jar. He gave the skin and the blood to Claudia. He threw the body in the Tiber River. Claudia hung the skin in an unused upstairs room that had a lot of sun to let the skin dry as quick as possible. She poured the blood out on in a wooden trough she had carried up there.

When both had sufficiently dried she had a trusted slave grind both into fine powders. The powdered skin she would drink in glasses of wine. The dried blood she mixed with ground red lead, ochre and red chalk to make her own rogue. The girls at the ladies only gatherings remarked at how clear her skin looked and, what oh what, was the secret to the orange tint in her rogue. Claudia kept her beauty tips to herself.

Caesar Sends Word

"Dear there is a messenger from Caesar in the garden. He looks like he has been traveling hard. I gave hime something to eat and a cup of wine. He insist on seeing you right away."

"Centurion, sit, please sit. You have a message for me?"

"Yes sir. It comes directly from Caesar. He told me to give it to you personally. Here sir."

"What does it say dear?"

"Let me read it first."

"Caesar has offered me command of his calvary in Italian Gaul.

He wants me to raise two Turmas of equites along with a legion of infantry and get them to him as soon as possible. The Germanic tribes are attacking in force and he needs calvary and more infantry.The Centurion is to raise infantry while I raise calvary to assist him. Centurion you may use my home if you need while we gather men. When you are ready we will meet on the Field of Mars before marching to Caesar. I am to be his Master of Horse. He asked that I not go to the Senate but report directly to him. What do you know of this Centurion?

"Sir we were camped in Cisalpine Gaul gathering supplies to head South for Spain and we were attacked by wandering tribes of Germans who were heading South to raid in the Italian Peninsula. We have stopped them for now. There is a rebellion in Spain that Caesar was commissioned by the Senate to put down. We are under siege and can't move. That is all I know sir."

"Centurion my home is yours. Claudia come with me. We are alone now dear I will tell you what else the letter said. Caesar says to come quick. He also says to bring all the extra food and supplies we can carry. He says to plan for a long campaign. He will share his plans with me when I get there. He stated that I must come now. He needs my calvary and my understanding of his tactics to help him defeat these Germans. Time is of the essence before the Celts and Gauls decide to join the Germans."

Three days later. "Claudia the Centurion has moved to the Field of Mars. He has assembled the infantry with the help of the infantry officers. My equites are still coming in. I told the Centurion as soon as the infantry was ready to tell the officers they were to march to Caesar. I outrank them so there shouldn't be a problem. I will follow as soon as I can when all of my men have reported. I will catch up with the infantry as soon as possible; if I don't they is to go straight to Caesar's fort. I sent Caesar a letter with the Centurion explaining when I could be expected. As soon as we get near his camp I will hide the calvary and sneak into his camp alone to see how he plans to defeat the enemy."

One week later. "My dear I am moving to the Field of Mars. I have almost two complete Turmas and men are still coming in. I am leaving a Ducurion in charge to bring along any stragglers. I must march tomorrow. Go to the temples and leave sacrifices for Jupiter and Mars. I love you. I will send word as soon as I can. Give me a farewell kiss my love. Goodby." And with that the Master of Horse kissed his wife goodby, mounted his horse in his private stable in the back of his house and went to war.

SPQR

(Senatus Populus Que Romanus)

Three weeks later Lucious in the middle of the night and dressed like a German peasant was brought into Caesar's tent. "I see you made it friend Lucious. Tell me how in that outfit you made it past my guards without today's password."

"Still living like a common soldier I see. Of course. I was lucky the Centurion you sent to Rome was on gate duty and he saved me."

"It wasn't luck my friend. He has been there every night since his arrival in camp. I know you my friend."

"I should have known. You are always one step ahead."

"Now tell me how many men did you bring. I brought close to two Turma almost six hundred calvary and horses. There is another Turma of almost three hundred maybe two weeks behind me."

"Good let me show you the my map. So you can fully see my current situation. Look at the map and tell me your thoughts Lucious."

"My strategy would for you to let the enemy keep your army bottled up inside your fortifications while I harass the enemy from the rear. I will divide my forces keeping one Turma as a reserve to build new fortifications in a different location every three days. I will send two Turma in different directions to raid. I will allow my two calvary commanders flexibility, I trust both completely with the discretion to combine forces or to work independently. I will tell them to avoid big fights with large groups of enemy fighters only to raid and burn villages and farms. They will only stay two weeks in the field before coming in to rotate with the Turma building the fortifications. We will keep this up until we hear from you with two exceptions. Caesar if my scouts see that you are being overrun or starved out we will come."

"Excellent my friend. That is why I sent for you. You think like me in battle. Sleep now and sneak out tomorrow night. They have no siege engines. I think they will soon get tired and lazy and go back on the march. As long as they are watching me they are not up to any mischief. One more thing if your troopers run across any villages with plague gather a few bodies and throw them into their camp. Now tell me is all well at home? The Senate knows nothing I hope."

"Our wives are well and have joined forces with the other officers wives to keep themselves entertained. I told the Senate nothing and left Rome as soon as I could. I'm sure the Senate knows something is up. They have more spies than we do. They sent no messenger to my tent at the Field of Mars."

"I do miss my wife but there is a time and a place for everything, heh Lucious? This is the time of war and hopefully we can send for our wives soon. Enough of this talk. Go sleep. We must pray to the Gods my men do not suffer too much during this siege. They are tough men. They know their duty. The extra supplies the infantry cohorts brought will help to feed them instead of eating what we have stored here."

Lucious is the best. I am glad I sent for him. He is the right man for the job thought Caesar as he lay on a blanket on the floor of his tent staring at the ceiling. Caesar did not sleep much when at war. His mind would give him no rest until victory was achieved. We need to finish here and get to Spain to appease the Senate. Patience old boy, patience.

Caesar and Lucious plan was working as expected. The Germans wanted to leave to protect their families from the Roman calvary, some did. A month later when the time was right Caesar told the Centurion known to Lucious to sneak out and deliver him a message. On the Ides of Junius attack the Germans from all four quadrants. Then assemble all your calvary directly in front of our gate and attack.. We will come out in force. I will take the infantry to the left and you the calvary to the right. We will encircle the siege and when we meet again we will join as one large army to follow those fellows and finish them off.

The plan worked perfectly and they followed the Germans until dark before reassembling at the fort. Caesar rewarded the men by letting them loot all night and the next day. The soldiers liked orders like this and most of them got drunk on barrels and wineskins of good German beer and Roman wine. They were allowed to keep any prisoners as slaves to be sent back to Roman slave markets. Any gold or silver found was of course theirs to keep.

Caesar allowed the Army a week to forage and gather supplies before their march across the Pyrenees Mountains toward Spain. Caesar had explained to Lucious that a renegade Roman General by the name of Quintes Magna Thax had built an army of Carthaginians, Egyptians and Spanish mountain peasants and was challenging Rome's authority. The good news was that his army was falling apart. His foreign troops had rebelled because of the lack of spoils and were now just a wandering mob of bandits. His mountain peasant army had betrayed him also and were now organized raiding against both his army and Rome's settlements. These peasants were a bigger problem than the foreigners. Caesar looked his old friend in the eyes and revealed his real plans. "Lucious, I am going to put you in charge of an entire army. What I tell you now is between you and me. If anyone ask you do not know my whereabouts. You were given orders for Spain, you left and that is all you know. Caesar stared at his friend waiting for a response; when none came he continued. "I am taking two Legions and one Turma of calvary and going to Gaul. You will take the rest of the army to Spain. I want you to convince General Thax that it is in his best interest to surrender, If he doesn't, wipe him out and send his head as a gift to the Senate. After you have dealt with the good general kill or drive the foreigners out of Spain. The last and most difficult part will be the mountain peasants. They hide in the mountains then regroup to attack before separating again to hide in their mountain hideouts. Find them and kill them and their families until they want peace. Show no mercy. Win or die are your orders.

Espania

Lucious took his army of consisting of one Legion of infantry and two Turma of calvary and crossed into Spain. His scouts assured him General Thax was in Italica with his army. Lucious went personally to General Thax headquarters to explain the situation the general was in. The Senate wanted his head. The best Lucious could offer was for the General to return to Rome on his own to face the Senate or face complete annihilation by the combined armies of Lucious and Julius Caesar who's army was only a week behind his. The General had no idea that Lucious was bluffing and Caesar was headed for Gaul. The General chose diplomacy over valor and turned his army over to the command of Lucious while he made post haste to Rome to try and save his head from resting on a spike.

Lucious combined army now was two Legions and two Turma of calvary. He released and thanked any and all mercenaries that had remained loyal for their contributions then had his men escort them to ships awaiting there departure. Lucious called for Thax's officers and asked for a detailed report on the location of the renegade Carthaginian and Egyptian rebels. Lucious sent his scouts with General Thax's to find the enemy. After the report was made

Lucious released General Thax's scouts but told his scouts to stay for a moment longer. As soon as the other scouts were out of range Lucious asked them their opinions not only of the scouts they were working with but the men from the new Legion that had joined up with ours. Lucious cautious as ever wanted no trouble makers or rebellion in the ranks. The scouts reported that their scouts were excellent and the troops in general were glad to be away from their rebellious commander. Good, good, thought Lucious.

The scouts said the foreigners looked to be disorganized and sometimes separated to attack different villages. They would raid a village, rape, steal, kill and take slaves then move on. They appeared to be slowly headed for the coast, most probably to take ships home with their haul.

Good, tell the mapmaker what you know and help him draw a map from where their army is and the location of all the villages between them and the coast. Two days later Lucious had his map and devised his plan.

He told his infantry commanders to march for the coast and where to camp and what to watch for. Lucious divided his calvary into two units to harass and drive the enemy into his trap. The enemy played their part as if on a giant stage with Lucious as the director. His army slaughtered theirs in a pincer movement. His army took all of their spoils including their slaves. Lucious provided his men with ships to send their slaves to the markets of Rome. This act helped to install even more loyalty to their commander. Lucious then turned his attention to the mountain warriors that had been harassing his rear.

Lucious had two choices either play the peasants game or the peasants could play his. He told his commanders to play along with the mountain people's strategy of hit, run and disband. Chase them but not too hard. Try to keep our men as safe as possible. Soldiers like to hear this from their commanders. A commander that did not waste his men's lives was a man to trust at least as long as the spoils of war kept coming in. In the meantime Lucious laid his trap. Lucious carelessly mentioned to his officers, being sure local slaves would overhear, about a huge gold shipment coming form Rome. It was backpay for the troops. It was a huge amount. The utmost secrecy was required. He quietly had already sent a cohort of calvary back across the mountains to return with oxcarts of wooden crates filled with lead. He then acted as if the backpay was on the way and a big celebration was in order. The trap was set.

Soon the word was put out the money was on the way. Lucious sent his infantry to hide until his scouts reported the mountain warriors had gathered and rode out in force out of their lairs to steal Rome's gold. As soon as the mountain warriors were clear of the mountain passes the infantry came out of their hiding places and put themselves amongst the rocks on both sides of the only pass that led to the mountain warriors villages. They blocked the only exit to the pass. Ass soon as the warriors entered the canyon they were attacked from both sides. Another cohort was waiting in the rear to close the entrance to the canyon. The mountain warriors were completely boxed in. Kill them all and then proceed to their mountain villages were the Legions' orders. Take whatever or whoever you want. The mountain force was wiped out to the man. Their villages strongholds were obliterated their women raped and the best still alive taken as slaves

Lucious sent word to the Roman Senate that Spain was secure and once again safe for Roman settlement. The Senate sent the message that a Triumph would be held for him and Caesar as soon as they returned to Rome. They were ordered to return to Rome as soon as possible to receive their reward. Why haven't we heard from Caesar? Sorry, Lucious thought, I work for Caesar not you band of thieves.

Vercingetorix

Lucious kept his army in Spain. He had sent word to Caesar in Gaul of his victory. He sent three different riders hoping at least one would get thru. The Senate had turned from being polite to demanding their return. Lucious trained his men and waited. Four months later he received word from Caesar that his plans were going well and he was pleased with his friend's success. He imagined nothing less. Trust me my friend. Keep stalling the Senate and soon I will send for you for the final victory in Gaul. We will not only be the most famous soldiers in Rome but I promise you my friend also the wealthiest beyond your wildest dreams. Gaul is full of gold and slaves for the taking.

Nine months later Caesar's messenger arrived with the long anticipated orders to join him with his army in Gaul at a place called Alesia. The messenger would guide him there. Lucious knew he was going against the Senate by following Caesar so before leaving he told his officers that if any of them or their men wanted to return to Rome they were free to do so. The entire infantry decided to stay hungry for spoils. About half a cohort of 150 men of the calvary returned to Rome, more afraid of the Senate than Caesar. Lucious marched his army north to Alesia. Two months later they arrived in Alesia; as was Lucious habit he sent his scouts forward to first find Caesar before advancing his whole army. Two weeks later his scouts returned with word to come to Caesar's aid. Once again friend Lucious hide your calvary away from prying eyes but send your infantry now. I have the enemy trapped in his capital and am building siege works. I can use the additional manpower of your Legions.

Upon seeing the completed fort circling the town. Lucious breathed a sigh of relief. Caesar welcomed him as a long lost brother. He told him to rest his men as they had much work to do.

He invited Lucious to join him in a cup of wine then it was back to work. "My friend the work here is only half done."

"I don't understand."

"We are going to build another ring of fortifications around these."

"Sorry. What?"

"Yes, I have Vercingetorix trapped inside. He has sent his scouts to gather his people. I am expecting another one hundred thousand to two hundred thousand warriors to attack us from the rear. Leave your infantry here to help build fortifications. Our combined armies except your calvary will remain here between the two walls. I will personally lead an action force to where the action is the hottest. Let me show you my drawings. I have deliberately left an opening in the outside wall. Vercingetorix scouts and spies will no doubt see it. That is where their huge army will attack. You must keep your calvary hidden from prying eyes. Kill all who get near. My whole plan relies on you my friend. Have your scouts watch closely and as soon as the savages attack. you attack from both flanks while I battle the front. Have both of your Turma work toward the weak spot I showed you. We will fight our way out to meet you. I do not think it will be long before they will be here. See those scarecrows and bodies lying about between here and the town? They are the women and children from the town. Smart bastard sent them out to save his food for his troops. Those men are watching their families starve in front of their eyes. It won't be long now."

"My friend you are either mad or a genius. I am here. We will fight. Tonight we will kill an ox as a sacrifice to Jupiter and Mars and we will wait for their attack. I wish us both good luck this time. Death or Victory."

"Death or Victory, friend Lucious." Caesar called very few people friend!

Caesar was not mad. He was a genius at war. After the defeat of his foe, Vercingetorix, Caesar took him to Rome in chains for his Triumph. The Senate had decided Caesar was a danger not only to the Republic but more importantly to them. They vacated the capitol after Caesar crossed the Rubicon River with his army. Caesar could have cared less. He created his own Senate and gave himself a Triumph parade thru the streets of Rome. The people of Rome loved him for it. He had taken his closest aide, General Mark Antony with him and left Lucious in charge of things in Gaul. Lucious sent for his wife to come to him. He had not seen her in three years. Seven months later her carriage arrived with news from Rome.

Egypt

Claudia arrived with bad news. Caesar was dead, assassinated by the Senate. Mark Antony was in Egypt. Soldiers were not far behind her to arrest her husband. They must flee. "No.", was Lucious reply to her demands. "They want me not you. I will flee to Egypt to join Antony with those of my army who want to go. You will take my share of the loot from Gaul and under escort return to Rome. But first things first. I haven't seen you in three years but you look as young as when I left you. How do you do it?"

"A woman's secret,", replied Claudia. She had already spied a beautiful young blond girl slave she insisted on taking back with her. She was running low of the powder that kept her face so young.

They spent three of the most passionate days they had ever spent together before parting, Lucious and his few loyal troops to Egypt, Claudia with her large entourage to Rome. The rest of his army waited for orders from the Senate. They men didn't mind. Whatever the future held they would welcome it, wealthy in gold and slaves. He promised he would see her again. Neither new it but Claudia was pregnant.

Antony was more than happy to see his old comrade. He inquired if the rest of his army was coming behind him. When Lucious told Antony the men he brought with him was it. He could tell by the expression on Antony's face he was disappointed. "We will make of it what we shall. I have told my Queen, Cleopatra about you. We are glad you are here. I know your work. I am going to make you the General of my land army. Cleopatra and I will maintain control of the Navy. We are working on a plan to defeat that young prick Octavian. You will be a vital part of my plan. I have told my officers and the Gypos you are now in command."

"Thank you Antony. I will get together with your officers and then see to my troops."

"Good, good. I knew you were the man for the job." and with that Antony disappeared to be with his Queen, his children and his opium.

Lucious talked this officers publicly as soldiers at meetings and privately as men. He went on an inspection tour of his troops. His officers were soldiers and would do their duty but none had confidence in Antony. He had been corrupted and influenced by the Egyptian Queen to the point he did whatever she suggested. There was no way this army could defeat a Roman army in battle. They also new the pair were working on some secret strategy with their Navy and ship building was going on at a rapid pace. They were gathering mercenaries from as far away as Greece. Lucious thought of his wife, his wealth and his unborn child and decided for the first time in his life to be a traitor.

He sent his messenger to Octavian in Rome and asked for a full pardon to live the rest of his life in peace in Italy for betraying Antony and Cleopatra. In return he would provide all of the intelligence at his disposal. He told the young man his greatest concerns should be at sea as Egypt was rapidly increasing its number of war ships to be under the direct command of Cleopatra with Antony as her advisor. Lucious was in command of the land army in Egypt. Octavian would have nothing to fear from his Army. Octavian sent word back to Lucious. He had a deal.

After the defeat of Cleopatra's fleet at Actium and the deaths of both her and Mark Antony Octavian true to his word welcomed Lucious back home. Lucious would never be allowed to hold a military office again but other that that he was free to come and go as he pleased. Octavian thanked him for his service to the state. Lucious, Claudia and their son Julius retired to Capri, built a huge estate and basked in the glory that was Rome.

The End

Made in the USA
Columbia, SC
30 October 2024